SCAVENGERS

SCAVENGERS

Issue 1.2

Edited & Curated by Shilo Niziolek

Querencia Press, LLC
Chicago, Illinois

"I was interested in the shape of the individual pieces. Some stories couldn't be told in an amorphous chunk of text. It just didn't work for what I wanted to say. Sometimes the world steers you towards the broken apart, the work that refuses to be glued together, that basks in its un-ness."

—Sinéad Gleeson, "Fragmented Narratives are Broken, Independent, and Honest"

CONTENTS

astrological analysis as alternative rock vs. indie folk
after "Drop Dead" [grandson] and "peace" [Taylor Swift], october 2021
—andrea lianne grabowski

"It's been eight minutes now. You need to text me back before you get to the subway and before I start driving or I'm going to be checking my phone on the 401 and for fuck's sake that's an illegal thing that is sort of dangerous.
Twelve minutes. I should try and be more secure than this. I really should. It would be good for me. Minomiinikeshii has unplugged her iphone and is making a new playlist because apparently I need it.
Fourteen minutes. It looks like this is turning into another opportunity to be brave."

— "Unsubstantiated Health Benefits," *This Accident of Being Lost,* Leanne Betasamosake Simpson

/ ♎ /15h / -15°/SQ3/538 sq. deg./+65°&-90°/ ♎ // ♓ /1h/+15°/NQ1/889 sq. deg./+90°&-65°/ ♓ /

in the advent of drifting off course/suspicion disguised as intuition/curses laid by those who came before including but not limited to, former selves with long hair and kool-aid stained neurons, do you:

    a.   be there, burning out
    b.   put the money on re[a]d
    c.   show no remorse
    d.   cash out
    e.   quit

answer: a - c. options d - e considered null and void, drop dead before choosing these answers.

15h 17m 00.41382s / -09° 22' 58.4919"

your scales hold the twin fish that swim in my chest
    but i do not know how to breathe air, and my gills

the seventh house, the house of balance,
    have never known enough water.
    some nights, all i see is the southern claw.

some nights, all i do is beg pardon for how

my saltwater has spilled from your copper plates.

but your tenderness is still a circumstellar habitable zone and

i will not atone for existence anymore.

the twelfth house was called the house of sacrifice.

but that is a deadname now.

4h 50m 41.18097s / -15° 59' 50.0482"

i'll send you letters spun from airwaves,

digital scrolls

with no expiration date.

    i am not patient.

    i fall asleep on a pillow of cords,
blue light my opium, always restless   for another fix.

—andrea lianne grabowski—

my plasma is fused from yearning. it may never be easy.

but for you, i

will try to weave gills of trust from

_x_ how we continue playing god with boys on a stage

_x_ the only moon to hold the mystery of an ocean

_x_ the only constellation to ever hold me.

i am becoming a dropout from the church of believing in my own undesirability,

falling on my knees before the godless surrealism of my fixed value,

of your endurance.

in the advent of unbalanced scales/falling into a faerie ring and losing agency over technology/fish drowning in their own lakes, do i:

a. swing with you for the fences
b. sit with you in the trenches
c. call a lack of total peace enough
d. give you my sunshine (stars are, in fact, suns, and suns are stars, and alpha piscium is but one of many)
e. waste your honor

answer: a - d. choosing option e runs the risk of fencing in the seventh house. lady justice is ██████ not an all-powerful god. therefore, do not treat them as such.

15h 17m 00.41382s / -09° 22' 58.4919"

maybe someday i will find a silver zippo lighter on the street.

spark all the bigotry till it burns bright as alpha piscium, beta librae —

55 +14/-11L☉X130L☉ and dies.

'cause it's not liberation while there's more churches than pride flags in this town.

rainbow balloons know nothing of hiding. they don't even know how lucky they are.

but for now, i will reach my head to rest

on your taller shoulder, in the safe luminosity

of a single, soft candle flame,

turned into a star by a 99¢ bic.

and is it not liberation until there's a word

for the way i love you?

but maybe we never needed a word

in the first place.

—andrea lianne grabowski—

FTD

—andrea lianne grabowski

i.

florists' transworld delivery

my father is being shaved.
he is roaring.
a boulder scrapes on another boulder.
dissolving chimney lurch in quebec woods.

falling whiskers—
his open mouth—
my mother's words—
neurons—
signals—
muscles—

sensationinstructioncomputationintegrationillumination   dead air.
the door alarms chirp like AI bugs.
i wish they'd sing *viiiiitamins,* make him laugh to tears.
the calendar reads *adventurous day* on april 15th.
new leaf/chapter/stage/any other cliche.

he flinches—
shower spray, pulled pork, vegan soup—
grumbling, whining—
everything but—
hot dogs and hugs—
thank god not hugs—

sensationinstructioncomputationintegrationillumination   dead air.

ii.

frontotemporal dementia

as the floral-gifting experts,
we've been helping.
we understand the unique power
of flowers to express.

established in 1910—
a floral wire service—
originally by telegraph—

the company utilized mercury—
flattened sketch of giambologna's—
sculpted god of—

speedcommercemessageseloquencetravelersboundariesluck   & communication.

all occasions bouquets. for example,
get well soon. the *hello sunshine* arrangement.
the *beautiful spirit* basket. let them know how much
you care. sunflower, delphinium, hydrangea.

we deliver to almost 100% of—
united states and canada—
for residential deliveries—
if the recipient is not available—
for business deliveries—
if the business is closed—

speedcommercemessageseloquencetravelersboundariesluck   & communication.

—andrea lianne grabowski—

Space Walk
   —Syd M.

The Star-Maker

—M.J. Walker

I shouldn't be in a job like this. The sight of blood affects me. When I was six I saw my mother cut her thumb while opening a can. Somehow the can slipped and the lid sliced through the fleshy part of her thumb right down to the bone. I remember how she gasped and lurched towards the sink, holding her arm out dead straight in front of her. Blood snaked down the length of that arm, way past the crook of its elbow. I was mesmerised by the sight of so *much* blood and wondered how much there was inside me. It was dripping from Ma's arm like a leaky faucet and falling in drops flamboyant red splashes on our new kitchen floor

Funny thing was Ma didn't cry out. She just stood there, mouth hanging open, eyes wide and staring, as drop after drop landed onto those shiny kitchen tiles. The tiles were azure blue, like the sky in high summer, and the splashes were red stars exploding.

'Get a towel,' Ma said in a weak little voice. She was taking in great gulps of air.

Ma's face was white as the line of clean washing I'd helped her peg out in the sun earlier that morning. I tried to move my legs but I found I couldn't. My sneakers were stuck to the floor. I think my mother must have fainted then because she sort of crumpled up before she fell. She went down gracefully in a single fluid movement and she didn't make a sound. It so happened, when she fell, though, that her skirt lifted up, showing off her pretty pink underwear. There were bloody patches on her apron and red smears like warpaint on her cheeks. I remember thinking she looked less like herself than an over-sized, under-stuffed doll.

I know what you're thinking but it ain't fair to judge. I do this job because I have to. I have a wife of my own and a family now, when all's said and done. It was two years ago I started here. It was part of a Wake Up and Work scheme. I'd been on welfare for some time before that so I was glad enough to get the chance.

For my first three months, they put me in the office. The work was easy but the take-home pay was a pittance. I stuck it out as long as I could and then I asked for a move. The foreman laughed and said *fat chance* but ten days later I was called to the office and found myself assigned to the Stun Team. The extra money came in handy but I found it pretty hard to adjust.

Technically, of course, there isn't much to it but what there *is* a build-up of tension. It eats away at your peace of mind and that sort of thing takes its toll. The thing is, they *know*. They *know* what's coming and the stink of their fear is unmistakable. By the end of a shift, that stink has found its way into your hair, your overalls, even your underwear. You scrub yourself raw in the wash house every night but you still take it home. Well, I couldn't afford to go back to the office so I decided to work my way out of there. I just put my head down and got on with it. I learned not to look at their eyes.

Now I'm here in Dispatch and Disposal. It took three months to get myself promoted. I make my bonus every week and the boss says I'm the best he's ever had. Doing this every day isn't easy for me but watching my kids starve would be harder. I do what I have to do. I do what I can.

Every once in a while, though, one comes along that reminds me of Ma in the kitchen. It's tough then and I'm not ashamed to admit to you, on those days, I cry. You see that look of terror in their eyes – even though, by then, they've been doped and stunned, some of them stay stubbornly conscious – and their scrawny old necks, stretched out and trembling, waiting for the knife like it's a blessing. Although I guess they must know it's no use struggling. What would be the point?

How does it feel? Well, let's just say you need a strong stomach. When you slide your blade across that puckered up flesh, you have to know exactly what you're doing. A firm, steady pressure, a nice smooth action. It's important to take your time. You feel the power of it then, pumping up your chest, and the blood blooms like a field of wild poppies. I can't begin to describe how I feel when that happens.

Sometimes the blood seeps and sometimes it spurts but, when it falls, it's like a galaxy of stars.

—M.J. Walker—

Garland Anchors Us In The Garden

inspired by 'The Blood Collages', by John Bingley Garland (England) 1850s

—Emily Tee

"I went to the Garden of Love,

And saw what I never had seen:

...

I saw it was filled with graves,

And tomb-stones where flowers should be:"

—The Garden of Love by William Blake

Walk with me in the Garden of the Tree of Good and Evil. It is now a cemetery commemorating the fall of mankind. The cherubim still protects the Tree of Life with its flaming sword, though you will only be able to see it against the cloudless perfect azure sky as if it was rendered in stone. Here among the beds that hold all of the flora of the earth that have ever bloomed and thrived since Eden's first blossoming are the burial plots, with many tombstones, markers and memorials. They rest among the oversized and fecund bounty of the natural world, just as they were when they were first planted. The ripe spilling fruits need no autumn, the luxuriant flowers blossoming wantonly need no spring as their vine-like stems grow and twine vibrantly. Now they form a backdrop to the monumental stonework depicting angels and seraphim who consort with holy knights and avengers. Only the most blessed can be interred here: prophets, saints and martyrs. Blood falls like tears, flowing for sorrow, repentance, redemption. The Christmas roses bear blood red berries, symbols of blood that was shed to atone for the sins of all. Crosses and ankhs pin everything in place under that unearthly red rain. The mood is sombre and still and few will breathe this rarefied pure air. The lasting feeling is solemn reflection on loss and faded glory.

—Emily Tee—

how to 'human'
  —Emily Tee

they make them look like girls

like attractive young women

they're less threatening, less scary that way

and people feel happier ordering them about

humanoid robots

artificial intelligence

they call it

stimulus-response

a machine-learning loop

but just the right things

specific tasks, activities

acceptable autonomy

we don't want this tool, this object,

to start forming opinions

having inconvenient needs

expressing its own ideas

outside the work assigned

we don't want it—her—

to start dreaming of her own destiny

imagining independence

Augmented and Virtual Reality
  —*K.G. Ricci*

—*K.G. Ricci*—

Backstory

—K.G. Ricci

Dead galaxies
  —Joseph Byrd

I found some of them while researching my bathroom.
Who is them? I ask myself. I adore that question.

I hope them are peacemongers.
I weep to see that word underscored as unrecognizable by my computer's brain.

Do not attempt to understand poetry. You will die.
Put down your need for understanding before it puts you down.

My 7th-grade daughter's first kitty cat did not understand that needle.
I can barely understand the language of her scream some eight years later.

How can I be sad when my children are so happy?
How can I miss what was my truest target?

Anyone else hear irony in the word carpool?
Soon it will be poolcar.

Hello mercury. You are risen indeed, and Jesus is getting jealous.
And then, my questions will start dripping off this page.

I can float with the best of them. I can tie balloons to my private parts.
Non-verified burglaries keep occurring in my pantry.

Soup is a relative term when the tide keeps rising.
Please don't assume you know which parts of me are private.

And some statuses should be stati. I have many of those going on within me today.
My current salary is based on my conversations with clowns. Please don't take me to any more circi.

I have been mocked by my progeny when I say iced tea or iced cream.
I am an expert at modifying my nouns, I shout back at their baby blankets.

Even if the nebulae expire, and the holes blacken beyond our understanding,
we can all say "I am that, I am there, too."

Just look in your bathroom mirror.
Just do the research.

—Joseph Byrd—

The Away Woman

inspired by her loved ones
—Phillip Hatcher

In the between dark. Below the achievements of a "modern age",
The skyscraper apartments illuminated in warmth and libation.
Materials grander than any old fortune. She fled.

Above the lit streets littered with late night wanderers.
Weekend warriors, bakers, and fishermen a-like
and the walkers walking only to keep warm, for sleep was worse.
Strugglin' with shopping carts and—

It was January during a cold snap when Miss B found
that sleep had become a lot warmer in that concrete corner.
The fourth floor of a parking lot had some kind of kindness
that was more accessible than all the turned away hands.

And we stand here still with an army of questions
not finding any treasure for answers.
Disregarding the ax next to the tree that lies across the road.

We found her in the morning.
Gone before she left,
when we finally took her in.
When we finally saw her.

—Phillip Hatcher—

Blue Million Miles

—The Pink Zombie Rose Project – Dia & Beppi

—The Pink Zombie Rose Project – Dia & Beppi—

The Captain knows this without ever leaving his post, which isn't high enough to see three blocks afield, but it's higher than the others, because your father got very annoyed with you at the end.

REMBEKA, THIS IS WHY A WOMAN GETS A MAN, BECAUSE ONE DAY IT HAPPENS WHERE HER BABA IS TOO OLD FOR FENCES.

If more men were like Baba, maybe you'd bother, but they all have big expectations, & yet they never inquire after your satisfaction. They don't attend to your body, let alone your fence. You said as much & Baba replied,

DO NOT HAND THEM A GLASS OR MILK FOR NOTHING. MAKE THESE SLOBS CRAWL UNDER THE COW & SHOW'EM HOW TO PULL THE TEATS.

He collapsed in the hammock laughing at his own jokes forgetting to chop the last post, which was another of his cosmic gifts, because that's how you met Captain Beefheart

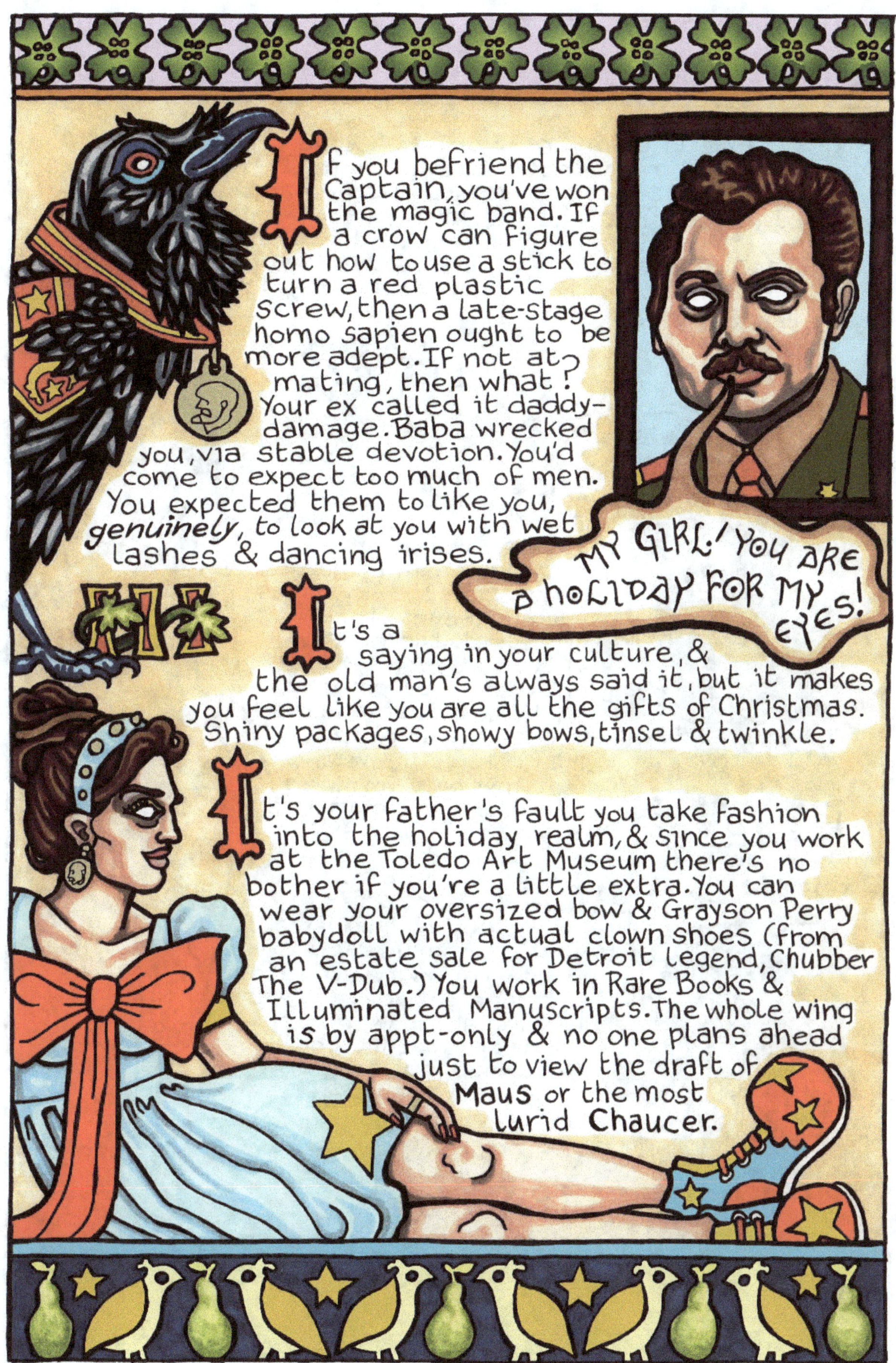

If you befriend the Captain, you've won the magic band. If a crow can figure out how to use a stick to turn a red plastic screw, then a late-stage homo sapien ought to be more adept. If not at mating, then what? Your ex called it daddy-damage. Baba wrecked you, via stable devotion. You'd come to expect too much of men. You expected them to like you, *genuinely*, to look at you with wet lashes & dancing irises.

It's a saying in your culture, & the old man's always said it, but it makes you feel like you are all the gifts of Christmas. Shiny packages, showy bows, tinsel & twinkle.

It's your father's fault you take fashion into the holiday realm, & since you work at the Toledo Art Museum there's no bother if you're a little extra. You can wear your oversized bow & Grayson Perry babydoll with actual clown shoes (from an estate sale for Detroit legend, Chubber The V-Dub.) You work in Rare Books & Illuminated Manuscripts. The whole wing is by appt-only & no one plans ahead just to view the draft of Maus or the most lurid Chaucer.

—The Pink Zombie Rose Project – Dia & Beppi—

You're the mistress of marvelous treasures, but no one even knows they're here. If it weren't for your elaborate plumage, you'd disappear into the pages (perhaps the bizarre DIY from the turn of the 15th century, where a monk details how to extract bovine semen, which he then fed to a mushroom all with the intention of ending the dark ages.)

No one cares if you pair a little black dress with an azure poodle, a balloon animal, worn like a jaunty hat. Anus first. Nobody minds your Museum of Fart turtleneck tucked into a red corduroy mini, + plus tights that you painted with Kusama dots. No one notices if your tulle skirt lights up: delivering urgent messages in morse code. They just grin like you were just any average Walgreens holiday—blinking ghost earrings or a xmas tree brooch. These so-called art lovers! It was the end of the day, twight, in midsummer, & you were pulling your trash can to the garage. You were blinking at dusk, no different that the fireflies, but Captain Beefheart noticed from the top of his post.

The Captain hopped down onto the neighboring post & called out to you. He recited the poem on your skirt, using a language of 5 sounds. Dah, di, dit, didy, didit. Then, in agreement: three dotty chirps, three elongated dashes, & three more dots. SOS.

Crows know the international symbol for distress.

While you were stunned at the time, it's not at all shocking to you now, as an honorary inductee into the House of Corvus. Or even to anyone who knows a goddamn. Immediately you were determined to become one of them, watching youtube videos until dawn, when you crept out with a box of fruit loops. Given your previous encounter, it wasn't hard to lure the captain. He followed the trail of colorful O's... but bypassed breakfast. He came to you directly.

When he tapped the poem into the picnic table, you tapped the next stanza. Per the poem, he causioned against love. You traded words & warnings. You give mixed nuts, they give bottlecaps. One day, you discovered a shiny dime on the corner of the picnic table & you realized that they understand not just fair trade but money—

—The Pink Zombie Rose Project – Dia & Beppi—

—The Pink Zombie Rose Project – Dia & Beppi—

(You don't mean to prevaricate, but you did see a box of hair dye in the kitchen trash. The rest is blonde: a dramatic effect.)

VITZI

DO YOU KNOW, THAT CHERNOBYL IS ALIVE AGAIN?

Nestle COLOR 'n TONE

NOW IT'S EVERYONE'S PROBLEM

He scolds you with an arthritic finger. Chernobyl is the family secret. Like everything he does, it's wise. People don't like proximity to disaster; at first, when there's press, when there's "human interest," but they fear survivors. They fear -& worship- the reanimate. He's frowning at the T.V. news -another virus. You confiscate the remote & cue up the video. Anarchist photogs sneak into a forbidden city before dawn. As the pink blackens, the landscape emerges. Chernobyl explodes in birdsong. Crows warn of trespassers. A rabbit chases a grasshopper. An enormous spider web stretches between two abandoned buildings. When a fox crosses a vintage carousel, your father gasps, because he remembers those painted horses. He believed the place had simply ceased to exist. If we couldn't go there, if not a soul lived there, then surely it must be lost to us forever. But here it is . . . .

СТІЙ! ЗОНА

—The Pink Zombie Rose Project – Dia & Beppi—

drift locket

—Monique Quintana

Crow tries to teach the prickle how to grow in the path of most minor affliction, but it refuses to listen. No matter how many crows talk, it believes it is most beautiful when hurting women's hands into curiosity and wonder. The prickle grew until it was a mountain top on the grapevine, ready to rupture and break cold blue dishes in the El Tejón diner. It interrupted the woman and her lover mid-kiss, and she spat in his mouth because they had lived in a drought since they were born, and she wanted to feel what cloudburst was like. Crow picks out bone fragments of his sister from the funeral pyre, and they drop in the bucket until they become blue dust. The birdling protests that she doesn't want to be contained in so small a thing; she wants to float down the river so the fish will believe they have entered another time.

Justifying Nature

—C.W. Bryan

In the park near my house they have tacked signs onto the trunks of decade old trees. I am not sure who "they" is, but I would imagine it's some genius at the Atlanta Parks Department. The Red Maple, for example, reads, "Red Maple, *Acer rubrum,* the seed is good for songbirds, squirrels, and small rodents; browse is good for deer; buds are good for squirrels." This development interests me on multiple fronts. There are points of interest on the flora and fauna front, but also on the anthropological front.

Now, I don't know what kinds of jobs exist in the Atlanta Parks Department. Frankly, when I think of clocking in to work at their downtown office I imagine either taking an 8-hour day to respond to emails of concerned citizens or hopping on a Segway and cruising through the Atlanta parks, keeping an eye on the urban sprawl. Whoever wrote this plaque (unfortunately, it was left unsigned) has an obvious love of nature. Nature probably loves him or her back, too. Afterall, the author refers to the tree by their Latin name, an obvious sign of familiarity, like the first time you ever call your childhood friend's parents Greg and Beth instead of Mr. and Mrs. Kilkenny. This is interesting to me, on the flora front. What is of interest on the anthropological side is the authority in which this author writes, "browse is good for deer."

This author writes with a chip on his shoulder, writes with the lexicon of a writer who wants to assert his authority through vocabulary alone. The author worries if he does not include words specific only to nature connoisseurs, we may not believe him. Though it seems natural to me that having the audacity to tack a metal plaque into a trunk implies all the authority one would need. For the uninitiated, browse, in this context, means "vegetation, such as twigs and young shoots, eaten by animals." Perhaps I overstate this plaque's intentions, but I would imagine they were placed into the trunks of trees at eye-level for the purpose of passing along some Red Maple trivia to an uninformed, park-walking audience. I wonder, then, if it would not have been more prudent to say, "twigs are good for deer", for the simple reason of allowing curious readers to continue their commune with nature without having to pull out their smart-phone-dictionaries.

This raises another question—what constitutes good? "Browse is good for deer, seed is good for songbirds, buds are good for squirrels." I wonder if the squirrels of Grant Park signed off on that. It reads to me like a parent planning healthy meals for their child. "Brussel sprouts are good for Jimmy. His 9-year-old body could use the nutrients," they say, as the kitchen begins to reek with boiled sprouts. Poor Jimmy doesn't get a say in what's good. The other week I saw a squirrel eating voraciously from a discarded Twinkie wrapper in the park. He was running and chittering in an elated state; I don't think I've ever seen a happier squirrel. Surely that Twinkie was good for his soul, if not his tiny rodent intestines. The plaque on the red maple justifies its existence based on diet. Perhaps I'll make a plaque of my own: "Hostess Twinkie, *Dolcis lignum,* the cake is biodegradable, the filling is good for squirrel's souls, the shiny wrapper is good for crow's nests." Justification at its finest.

Which leads me to the last bizarre aspect of these plaques—justification. What reason must the mysterious author in the parks department have to create this copy? "Don't worry park promenaders, this tree exists for a reason! Don't think for one second we would plant a tree whose browse was useless!" It all seems silly to me. The utilitarian bent of the Atlanta Parks Department surprises me. Nature is enigmatic, nature is a wonder. Nature is not dietary benefits, nor does it need explanation. I wonder if our mystery author read too much J.S. Mill and not enough Emerson. Emerson would have been a great copywriter for the Atlanta Parks Department—I can imagine his first plaque now: "The lover of nature is he whose inward and outward senses are still truly adjusted to each other; who has retained the spirit of infancy even into the era of manhood. So stop reading, pull your socks and shoes off, and walk through the park with eyes closed."

—C.W. Bryan—

Portal
 —Rachel Mulder

—Rachel Mulder—

Sentinels
—*Rachel Mulder*

—*Rachel Mulder*—

Gli Angeli
 —*Rachel Mulder*

 —*Rachel Mulder—*

She Makes No Sense
—Adrianne Reig

I loved her, so I needed to see her bones. She was always doing things that made no sense, like leaving bundles of lavender and vervain on the hood of my car and giving me strips of willow bark to chew on and keeping all the spiders I killed in a jar on her nightstand and if I asked her to buy apples, she wouldn't do it, and one night as we lay in bed I told her maybe I'd be able to understand her if I could just see her bones, and she laughed at me but the next day we went to the hospital to get her an x-ray and the doctor said there was nothing wrong with her bones and she put the pictures up on the wall to show us and I said no, no, something is wrong, I'm sure of it but the doctor said ma'am she's fine, I promise, and I didn't say it out loud but I thought, I love her so much, something has to be wrong and we went home that night and she hung the x-rays over our bed to remind me her bones were okay and we went to sleep and the next morning I told her that's a pretty necklace you're wearing but it was actually her collarbones poking out through her skin and I kissed them both and said I'm so glad to see you and her bones kept popping out all over until she wore her skin like a shawl and soon it fell away and I wasn't quite sure whether I should talk to her skin or her bones but her skeleton clattered to the floor and I picked up every one of her bones and examined them one at a time and just as I was about to put them back together they changed shape in front of me, bending and twisting into curlicues and spirals and I panicked and tried to bend them back the way they were before but they snapped and shattered between my fingers and lay around me in twisted shards and there was nothing I could do, nothing at all, and I told her I'm sorry, I'm so sorry, and her skin was too full of her blood and guts to move so I let her lie there and her mouth and her eyes were empty and the worst part was I still didn't understand her. But I still loved her and despite what had happened, I was glad I'd seen her bones.

—Adrianne Reig—

Like The Moonrat I Am Crepuscular
—Abigail Ottley

I am pointy-snouty, a scourge among insects. cousin to the mighty hedge-pig. Not mouse or a rat so do not mistake me. Though I am but little I am fierce. Like the golden mole I hold in close kinship, my vision is sadly defective. My nose, though, is keen to twitch, my claws, my incisors, sharp as spikes. Like the moonrat, I am crepuscular in nature. I will forage in the shadow of the owl. My appetite is such I will eat my own weight, then eat myself again. I betray no fear in defence of my home. I will battle mighty giants and slay them. Though my teeth weep poison I kill by crushing. I can make a skull snap like a twig. A prudent lover will ponder on this, will not look lightly to pet me or to tame me. I will be no man's hawk or wet-eyed spaniel. I am Sorax araneus. I bite.

*The common shrew is the second most numerous British mammal, most recently estimated at 41,700,000.

—Abigail Ottley—

Remember the air

—Abigail Ottley

Remember the air in that far-flung country/at all costs/remember it/ remember /even as the gun is raised/ glossy/gleaming with new oil/see how the vast dizzy sky/ flashes blue then gold/in the moment of the barrel's slow alignment/ remember how grass smells green and earthy/hopscotch and handstands/dragonflies and mayflies/how buttercups dance under your chin/remember now/in the moment/before falling/how this muzzle obtrudes /a winter finger/ rigid/cajoling/ nuzzling/nuzzling like a lover/caressing the curve on the zygomatic bone/ below the gape and stretch/of your eye/remember the air in that place /where you were/it is fragranced/by the sweet scent of lilac/ remember how your nana/ wagged her hooked finger/ said not to bring wild lilac indoors/

Bird In A Net
—*Abigail Ottley*

Caught in a mesh of whispered words,
wingless, beak-stifled, mute,
my feathers are silky, smooth as your
 promises, star-lit by shivers of sky.

Feathered for flight, I am lustrous, unruffled,
yet mastered by your pale crooked finger.
Soon you will pucker your bloodless lips,
 coo your supper-time prayer:

There, there chickadee, come to daddy.
Come lightly on your hollow bones and feathers.
Come, come. No harm shall be done.
Nestle yourself on my knee.

—Abigail Ottley—

Girl-Bird in the World of Dreams
  —*Irina Tall (Novikova)*

—*Irina Tall (Novikova)*—

field notes

—*Kristin Yates*

feathers, antlers,
stray kernels

of corn.
white clover,
honeysuckle air.

branches,

snapping.
songs and

calls.
slivers of

fur, bark,
seed.

tracks.
musk,

wet mud.

half-open
nut husks,

holes
in the ground.
eyes,

listening.

pollen dust.
ears,

gazing.
prints

in sidewalk.
evidence

we are here,
too wild

to be held.

—*Kristin Yates*—

Amelia
—*Kristin Yates*

as the sun rose
she

eloped to

a

blue
sky,

and

she   made five different kinds of

creatures,

who

cared for us

at her grave

—*Kristin Yates—*

Alice in the bath

—Kristiana Reed

Thoughts pervade, on par with cymbal clatters and the dishes you've left for too many nights and the potato starch has attached itself, limb by limb, to the pan. One dream circles, once and round again. In the middle of a day—a daydream-noon—I find myself rooted to the spot. I find myself staring up, bleary eyed at an old terraced house, indistinct in its architecture; it could be any period; it could be freshly painted and the paint peeling in sunburn flakes; I could be anywhere. Yet, the sun shines high and blissfully ignorant.

A little girl waits for me. Her dark eyes usher me onwards before her hands clutch mine, leading me forward into the middle townhouse. The paint peels, sunburn and skin. And she disappears. A shadow, a figure, a flimsy strip of black lace disintegrating into the damp mottled walls. But in the dark, her hollow eyes follow me and lead me simultaneously.

Thoughts pervade, on par with nightmares dressed in silk, washed in honey and milk.

A mother—my mother, perhaps—smokes and stirs a bubbling pot above a blue flame. The room smells like a funeral; chemical and floral. Goodbyes fermenting as rotten fruit. We eat in strange silence in the presence of men—faceless and nameless. Dark eyes settle and sink. My skin itches. Peels. Sunburn.

One girl sleeps downstairs, I hear her voice as she sings and strums. Minutes pass and an ecstasy is reached.

A mother smokes, tips back her head and laughs; inhales pheromones and the hearts of men.

I feel mine palpitate as my skin shrinks closer to the bone, clammy with night sweat even in a daydream-noon. This dream circles—vulture-like—above my head. The weight of an albatross, clinging like muggy air, around my neck.

The only light emits from the stove's blue flame, the static television—kaleidoscopic black and white— and the upstairs hallway. I ascend the stairs. Float towards the back bedroom with a lock on the door and no windows. Light flashes across a screen and the motel quality light bulb swings by my head. There is a bed, a desk, and a bath already full. Dull dishwater. Scum lines around the edge but the heat invites me. I descend—fully clothed—I shrink. Alice in the bath.

My sleeves constrict around my wrists; my breasts wither to pinpricks, cold in the evening; my jeans cut my ankles but the water is so warm. I cup my palms, lift the water to my lips like brandy and knock back the memories held in each soapy bubble. But there is no soap and I remain unclean—shrinking sopping wet.

The weight of an albatross, clinging like damp to mouldy walls, around my neck.

I sink—submerge myself—swallow the bath like the sea and wonder why I am here. I wonder why I do not have a home and why the hallway light is so bright and why I never hear the mother—perhaps, my mother—come up the stairs. My cries echo in porcelain. A daydream-noon.

—Kristiana Reed—

Dreaming
—*Andi Benet*

—*Andi Benet*—

Dream Thieves

—*Kenneth Johnson*

The palms looked like crepe paper flowers in the stifling heat, the chain-link fence like wings of a broken bird. What was left of a front lawn made the old wooden house look abandoned. She sat on the front porch while scanning the neighborhood for a glimpse of the intruders, thieves on wanted posters archived in her now impenetrable vault. She sat on her front porch every afternoon, sipping strong black coffee, hoping to spot the criminals who stole her dreams. She had kept them under her pillow at night while waiting for the Dream Fairy. She recalled the times they broke into her home over the years. It didn't happen all at once. They chiseled away bit by bit, like master sculptors carefully following their preliminary sketches and well-crafted maquettes. One night, their work was completed, and they moved on. She figured they were most likely in one of those luxury townhomes in the mirrored high rises she could barely see on the distant hills overlooking the city. They were probably laughing, dining, watching big-ass televisions, and saying things like *my god, look at that view.* When she closed her eyes, she could see them talking about the meaning of life. They had moved on, but they'd be back. She was sure of it.

Bit Parts

—Kenneth Johnson

He boxed up his memories,
all his secrets, and returned
to his rural hometown after
decades of fruitless auditions
for various roles,
          mostly bit parts.

On the road, he thought about
a Samurai sword exhibition
he saw in a show at a hospital
he visited on a trip to revisit
places where he had been
          stationed in Japan.

Once home, he began to clear
the land of debris and trash,
dead shrubs and diseased trees.
He felt renewed. One evening,
he sat on the porch to marvel
     at his progress.

In fading light, he recalled his mother
taking him and his sister to pick
wild blackberries by the creek,
long since diverted for some reason
          no one could remember.

—Kenneth Johnson—

Begin
—*Cyrus Carlson*

—*Cyrus Carlson*—

Answers

—Cyrus Carlson

—Cyrus Carlson—

sieve

—Gerald Majer

" shedding its skin as it swims creating the river through which it is moving"

—Gerald Majer—

1.

All like, they grow all over us, these organs of expropriation, these annex limb phantoms, the house, the automobile, the wife, the husband, the child under pressure, under pressure, under pressure.

2.

In the dream, the phrase "fountain excision," and I'm all like, oh, remember this, remember this!

3.

All, all, all—what the Fountain says.

4.

On the country radio a song about party mode, another song about a wonderful love who sings along with every song on the radio and I want this night never to end with our immortal endless highway run wey arc out the windows.

5.

The new ones move in and they one day squirt with hoses in the sun and their bare skins shine.

6.

The thing about las fuentes is that the flow flowers from itself and gives itself away to air and noise and las fuentes mean that everything only happens with this giving away, the part that seems to throw itself away is the part the rest of everything is possible from.

Agamben, the philosopher, the times he talks about uses—every use, say, of this paddle to strike this ball, holds back something—that's the fountaining of it.

7.

"Intellectual thought, emotional knowledge, and kinetics or movement"—Leanne Simpson talks about the three proximate and together and they are getting all fountainous.

~~~~~~~~

I wake up and the sun is in my apartment sitting on the couch with their legs scissored.

—Gerald Majer—
~~~~~~~~

I can't see the legs exactly because even though the disc is shrunk and the temp is way down the thing still is super bright.

I ignore it and go right past to the kitchen and drink a glass then two more glasses of water, it's that dry in here with it blazing.

I feel like crying, real weeping, because the sun is blazing in here and shining out of my window but the blaze is already fizzling a little. And the sun not shining in through the window. It's only in here shining a miner's lamp melting inside a fire.

The world outside is dark. A million headlights and streetlights and floodlights on but the dark is heavy so they are little sparks in a tar vat.

With sirens going, lots of bonfires and street fires also looking drowned under pressure from the dark.

My place has the star. There's a touch of light on the wall of the apartment building across the street. Coming from my window.

I hear other people weeping, screaming.   Someone is yelling like he's high.
It's 730 in the morning. Sirens are close, right in front, a helicopter is over my building circling.

They know the sun is in here.

I look at the thing sitting on my couch and it still blazes. My eyes are dazzled. I'm getting sweaty. Thirsty again. I want to throw myself on it. Save the sun. Love the sun. Keep the sun from getting away.

Doom patrols are pounding on the stairs and down my hallway. The door breaks down and they clang over its panels like it's a space bridge.

At close range your brain shuts down vision but the sun makes you hallucinate, scientists will determine later. I'm seeing golden flowers and silver limbs. I don't want to. Give me the real sun but it's said no one can bear it. Seeing dinosaurs, cupcakes, eyes in pyramids. It goes rawly erotic. It goes into drug colors, half blood, half glitter.

This shit seems vast as the end of the world.

The soldiers get lost approaching the couch.   Some believe they are in a tunnel. Others are singing like the victorious ones.

I believe I'm a little kid and I go and take the sun by the hand. Our hands together swing a little.   It feels impossible to be friends but the fiery hands keep swinging.

Now I have to go out and introduce my new friend to every single person in the world, one by one.

They get light on them and it catches.

A good big plague might save us, we think, but the shadows on our hands are thick as the black between stars.

—Gerald Majer—

We squeeze out the shadows in steamy hand fountains.

~~~~~~~~~

You're not looking at anything at all here. A line is conjuring across. The arc of it you can't get fixed. The inside side may be the outside side. The thing probably has its own weather. Islanded. The brush with the flows slides off whatever memory is left. A spring winding down inward, a lever taking off steep.

Tenderness, come guess. What's around toward the round and the circle. The excuse for the limbs, the arms, and the legs to be flying out from there.

Or proposing that a fastest spin verges on a point standing still.

Momentum would be easier than animation, which is always requiring that it live and give.

Cannot hold the thing only stone. Water draping rain. Motors faking rest.

You're wondering if each object you don't know is tracking, sniffing. Not a hunt here but a long breathe.

Or this is a pot loosened from crosshatch and spiral. It doesn't hold or holding this time means pouring itself in. The world around it thirsty to be touched, which is why it's a world anyway.

~~~~~~~~~

1. An intersection of two laterals, of two planes: the floor of the winnowing pan with its perforations, the slide of the shucked corn over it.

2. Lucretius, the clinamen, the swerve: all the particles falling and here and there the fall turns, moves. Lateral plane of the falling, lateral plane of the move, the swerving away. Everything we inhabit, world and time and space, happens right there and then.

—Gerald Majer—

3. SIEVE from PIE **seib-* "to pour out, sieve, drip, trickle" (see *soap* (n.)). Related to *sift*. The *Sieve of Eratosthenes* (1803) is a contrivance for finding prime numbers. Sieve and shears formerly were used in divinations.

4. A sieve is also a called a *riddle*. Let this collaboration be an exploration of why this is so. A riddle is a sort of hole, holes? The riddle's answer is sifted out from it, or shaken out from it.

5. *seisesthai*—the shaking of the sieve, the shaking out, sifting out motion, where there's something happening but the sense of any place where it's happening seems suspended, indefinite—this is an aspect of the chora, the primordial medium or space where all things come to appear in existence— "The tremor in the course of which a selection of the forces or seeds *takes place* (and this makes PLACE itself, where everything happens).

6. Democritus—atoms move only because the void cedes space to them, atoms alone can do nothing, they are just an immobile mass.

"Primordial spatiality," the productivity that is required for the diacritic proto-temporalizing movement that is spacing, in the chora, the chora—

which is a kind of active void;

"Atoms had no movement of their own; it was by the differential adaptation to the void of their forms and their sizes that they were carried in all directions. One source states "[the atoms] glide in the void, which, by not offering any resistance, is equivalent to a proper movement." (from Louise Burchill)

7. The sieve is the void. It doesn't let things fall through holes. Rather, the sieve makes a PLACE (like a plane) where the things being shaken and tossed find their shape.

~~~~~~~~~~

It's all this foam hair

the washy glitter receding
the crotchy trenches
the molten troves

and the stuff all about itself
in spiny mouths

wey get the dappled stippled
welling part

—Gerald Majer—
~~~~~~~~~~

wey get the sun foil
on raised water knees part

wey get the tangled part
the piece where it strands

all unwoven
(look at that stuff not stopping
as it's always just finishing up)

though the part with all and all
wey don't get, wey fear the word
unless wey stand right under it

and it fucking hurts everywhere.

—Gerald Majer—

Preface

—Alex Rodberg

—Alex Rodberg—

PABULAR PHONIES

—Alysa Levi-D'Ancona

Paper, plastic, petroleum, Malia penned as she pursed her lips. She held the neck of her pen delicately between her middle and ring fingers, guiding the force with her thumb. She considered the color choice of her nails, adoring the understated pink of Essie's Starter Wife, but wondering if the vibrancy of OPI's Ladies and Magenta-men would've better highlighted the attention to her notetaking.

Laila scribbled furiously in her notebook: *Porter's wheelhouse is a metaphor, no, an allusion to the family structure as a result of the exigence of first wave feminism.* The words took on a slant nearly eighty-five degrees to the right, but she needed Professor Pottins's words, needed them in the exact form that they catapulted with spit past his yellowed teeth. *What wave are we on now? Doesn't matter.*

Pottins's sigh rattled with the phlegm caught in the back of his throat, an annoyance that popped up sometime after his third daughter, Lisa, started biting him in his sleep. Wendy insisted that co-sleeping would help Lisa's night terrors. "And it's only temporary," she'd said. When Lisa began teething, though, she found his fingers in their bed and never Wendy's. Maybe it was the thick, black hairs that combed over his digits. He'd read somewhere that babies had affinities for these things: hair, dirt, excretions. He rubbed his fingers now, at the front of the lecture hall, finding fury and comfort in the scabs along his hands.

Right, so, the hegemony of the, the, we are all—Sit down, Mr. Singh. Thank you. Laila would be prepared for the final, of course. With these notes—she was almost tearing up with pride—there was no way she could miss anything worth evaluating on the exam. And with Professor Pottins as her advisor, she would receive a glowing recommendation for her PhD program. She just had to get his attention somehow. *Now, where was I?*

Malia turned to look at Josh, the lacrosse player whose text messages buzzed in her pocket. Sure, she let him tongue her in exchange for an essay or two, but it wasn't like it was her idea. He offered, nearly begged to do all the work for her Tuesday-Thursday chemistry class. Who was she to say no, especially when she had other matters she'd rather attend to? *Pomegranate, plum, pickle.* Malia drew an arrow through the *pickle* and smiled at her own private joke.

What did the young woman in periwinkle pajamas in the front row think she was doing, laughing at him? thought Pottins. He noted the pink pom pom on top of her pen bobbing slowly with the curvature of her writing, which was far too meticulous to be taking down any of the notable things he'd said since the lecture began. What a leisure it would be to have such a devil-may-care attitude. He bet she even slept. This was what his life had come to, he thought: chew toys and background noise.

Chew toys and background noise, Laila noted, furrowing her thin brows. A drop of blood splatted onto her notebook, she assumed from her lip, which she'd been biting in concentration. But she didn't have a spare moment to check, to pay heed to the tingling in the back of her throat, nor to process what her classmates had realized: that Pottins was sprinkling his thoughts into the lecture. *Although Geoffrey speaks in platitudes, it is what he doesn't say that, as a protagonist, that speaks to his characterization. He is nothing, nothing at all to the minor characters of the story. And for that reason, even though he overspeaks, he never really is heard. Familiarity, a funny thing.*

—Alysa Levi-D'Ancona—

Platitudes, protagonist—Malia searched the air for a third word. What was it called when someone's words and actions didn't match…? Ah, right. *Personal inconsistency.* She frowned at the failed parallelism of the phrasing. Oh, that would do, she realized. She crossed out *personal inconsistency* and instead wrote *parallelism.*

A frown now? Pottins's words escaped him faster, a fury tickling his tongue as it flew through syllables and consonants. Pottins wanted confirmation that the pajamaed girl was anywhere but engaged. Sure, he would've liked to join her in his own escapism—away from his home and the university. He'd authored seven books and was invited to Caryl Churchill's house, for Christ's sake.

Laila sneezed loudly. She caught viscous boogers in her palm as she covered her nose. In a panicked flurry, she dove into her backpack for tissues. When she wiped down her hand and face, she froze, realizing she had stopped penning the accelerating words of Professor Pottins. Launching a hand in the air, she continued scribbling. *…Never even considered the revelation of the penultimate swan. God, periwinkle? The audacity. Porter chose a sensible color, like green. Green like grass, trees, money. Money. That's why we're here. Money.*

Perturbed, plaintive, pathetic. Maybe Malia would get tacos al pastor once she revealed what she knew. More satisfying that way. A bite once she sunk her teeth in. *Puny, petite, pint-sized.*

Maybe Pottins would rent a hotel room for a week. A full week. Imagine that: a full night's sleep with no teeth at all.

The human mind can only contain so much information before it must discard it somehow. Laila had been raising her hand for three minutes now. She contemplated shouting his name, but then it would echo in the lecture hall. Would he know her name then?

Predictable, predicament, paradox. Fabular, phony, Pottins.

It would seem that some of us might relate to Geoffrey more than the wheelbarrow, and some of us to the wheelbarrow more so.

He couldn't explain why, but Pottins decided at that moment that this was the hill he was going to die on.

Excuse me, miss, but what on earth—?

Malia set her pom pom pen down as the professor stomped toward her notebook, leaning back in her onesie. Satisfaction filled her as his eyes glazed over, horrified at her work: *Phallic, photograph, pay me and pass me. Or else.*

Pottins couldn't tell what was more infuriating, the petulance of the pajamaed young woman or the fact that she couldn't even commit to her stupid fucking wordplay.

Laila lifted her head up from her paper at last, her subject silent. Why was he silent?

Malia knew he hadn't an inkling who she was, and she bet he wondered if it was her he'd slept with or another student. Women spoke with one another, Malia mused, and secrets never left the walls of a university, not really.

Goddamn Peggy, Pottins thought to himself. She'd broken up with him after Lisa was born, an undergrad lecturing him about morality only after he'd helped her get into Columbia's graduate program. And now she'd sent some lackey to blackmail him? The irony. Chew toys and background noise.

What did she miss during the sneeze? Laila cursed herself.

Malia heard the mousy "Professor?" from behind her, but her eyes remained locked on Professor Pottins.

As the rest of the hall stared at her in tense curiosity, Laila felt underdressed in her overalls and a messy bun. "Uh, professor? Can you repeat your comment about the penultimate swan?"

Sighing through rattled phlegm, Pottins turned to the blackboard, grabbed his leather briefcase, and walked out of the lecture hall.

—Alysa Levi-D'Ancona—

adaptation of Dua Lipa song where every heartbreak is an empty envelope in a Taco Bell restroom
   —Liam Strong

[don't start with unstudied taxa. don't with the *mollusca*, hermetic or aphroditic or. otherwise don't germinate in the ocean where the fish aren't plentiful. don't laminate. don't lick. don't bury the habitat you created. don't filter it all out, don't yearn, don't yearn because it spreads planktonic, don't with what you made unseen. don't with seeing the distinction between mantle & or mantle, don't with the exposure of earth for earth. don't end with flesh for flesh. don't say the sake it's for, sweet aragonite like taffy. don't with your chitin, ribbons filled with mouth, don't with words, don't word it like you would, don't tongue the wound when it isn't a wound. don't say yet. just don't.]

—Liam Strong—

self-emasculate tranny wins the arms race, puts an end to all human conflict, etc.
   —Liam Strong

hestian womb, squall line above their head, hestian scorched earth warfare, women's skinny

jeans with the tag surgically removed, size something, size unfit for tucking what must be hidden, for justification, proof, parent's blessing, fear that the unknown is what occurs beyond the word *fuck*, fear not cosmic or rheian or apollan or whatever the fuck, esophagus of torches curtained with tongue, prayer in spayed wood, floorboards sans the nails, the kind of superstition

that ends in neutering, the end-all-be-all worst, to think that anything could be that, inhuman, prefix inward like inversion, nudity a form of having formed, what isn't a housewarming gift, a knife, to think that bad luck isn't being fucked, loss of hestian virginity, bird of hermes gasping for wind, their blade licks at storms, even the earth is fucked, to think that anything that cuts

creates separation, which is just another method of castration

interrogation concerning your anorexic son, the one with the ponytail

> *after Kemi Alabi*

—Liam Strong

1. has he considered metal music?
2. do you think swapping pronouns at this point will help?
3. did you know Starvation Lake is only about 45 minutes from here, in Mancelona? it's also in Florida. & Utah!
4. we can't say the same for a glacier, no–why would it want to be warm?
5. exodus? numbers? according to WHO nutritionists, caloric energy cannot be created nor destroyed.
6. what if he started working out?
7. what if he played lacrosse? or hockey, even though it's past season? but not fencing. anything but fencing.
8. what if we got him a girlfriend?
9. when given the rorschach test, do you think he'll discover the ideal shape?
10. is he by any chance ambidextrous, eating with the wrong hand?
11. which foods take the longest to expire?
12. do thoughts count?
13. does the human body?
14. how many stale chips does it take for him to go numb?
15. what do you do with your bones when you're done?
16. will they return to our mothers?
17. will they become our mothers or fathers again?
18. when we're brought into this world, how much food is in our stomachs, if any?
19. have you told him nothing is not enough?
20. have you told him to disregard double negatives?
21. have you told him capitalization is a form of unjust praise, though we do it anyway?
22. is it too late to inform him of how life works?
23. how easy is it to reset the time on a stopwatch?
24. to begin again?
25. does he know it's not like construction, not like rebuilding?
26. that you just can't go changing yourself willy nilly?
27. maybe you can suggest religious fasting instead?
28. maybe what we have here is fungal, as if his body has been taught how to consume the wrong way?
29. maybe it's not rhythmic, without a circadian beat?
30. what's his metabolism like?
31. how does he convert sugar? is he getting enough meat?
32. have his English teachers said anything about man being an island or a desert or the like?
33. has he been having too many sleepovers with mirrors recently?
34. are you able to see him clearly?
35. & if not, what do you see?
36. are his breakdowns catabolic? metabolic?
37. can you tell the difference?
38. can you tell me which one is him?

—Liam Strong—

The Vibe

   —Ell Cee

something like that

—*Dallas Knox*

"I've known for a long time now…that I'm gay. Or something like that."

The car ride from Chattanooga to Nashville is the same as it's always been. The green mountains whiz past us on this nearly vacant highway and for a second it feels like we're flying. It's times like these when I feel the least real. This place without a place, it's mystical almost. This vacuum is where the driver, my mother, is forced to hear me. Nowhere to run, she's unwillingly confronted with the truth. My truth, as unstable as it is in all its glory, she's heard it now. Though the car is (un)comfortably silent I can barely sense her breaths over the static of my racing thoughts. I'm waiting for a response, for what feels like forever, but it must be in reality a few seconds. I have to suppress my urge to tuck and roll out of the car, afraid of my own words.

I think my lungs might collapse if I hold my breath any longer. I've said my part and it's her turn now. So why do I feel like this? Like as if her response will change something, as if it really matters. I'm done choking this down. I don't care what her response will be when the office ladies ask who I'm bringing home for thanksgiving, when she has to admit to her fellow divorcee friends that her daughter is a raging baby bull dyk—

For an infinite moment, I'm there again. Too small to see over the horizon of the golden oak of the pew and too little for my feet to reach the plush, purple ground. The gory paintings which line the wine-red walls remind me of the great sacrifice I so selfishly waste. I can feel their beady eyes watching as I step sheepishly down the aisle. there's a traitor, a sinner amongst us. I spend so much of my short life in churches like this in between believing in him or myself. I think a lot of non-religious people assume that a church is only physical, but it's much more than that. It's my grandmother, my girl scout troop, my teacher, and my youth pastor. Their expectations, their visions, their effigies of who I might be one day. They are (were) all my church. This unmoveable force of faith I am accustomed to is not unlike the Garden of Eden for God's first creations. As long as Eve remained untempted, she lived. As long as I keep my head bowed and eyes shut in the church, I can breathe.

How many times can someone be saved? How many times can I cry and shake and beg for forgiveness before God stops listening? He knows I cannot change, so why does he continue to make me repent for it? Why did he make Jesus feel the nails being hammered through his palms? Why couldn't it just be for show? Why does God like to watch us suffer?

I can pretend to breathe —at least in between the shaky recitations and tainted prayers. I'm late to Wednesday chapel again. My too-short school girl plaid skirt is giving me a wedgie and my knees are bruised from having the bottom locker in the 7th-grade hallway. I don't feel like "receiving the word of God" today, but still, I persevere singing my prayer songs with tight lips and a mind elsewhere. I can feel my out of placeness. It creeps up on me in times like this when the hairs on the back of my neck stand at attention during worship. When the holy spirit seems to lend its touch to everyone in the room beside me. When I'm barely able to swallow my bland communion cracker, like Styrofoam in my already dry mouth, and the too sweet grape juice the pastor has so kindly bestowed upon me. This feeling of uncollective effervescence strikes me the most when I let my thoughts wander. When I wonder what it'd be like to dance with another girl. Swaying softly from side to side with our cheeks pressed together, arms intertwined, praising one another.

—Dallas Knox—

It's beautiful really. How easy it is to love and be loved without a pastor peering over your shoulder, telling you what you feel is wrong. Without an ounce of guilt. That's a little optimistic. The guilt and shame is still there, but the difference is I am content with my fate now. Hell can't be any worse than how I was living before. If you can even call it living. More like waiting to be cured from a terminal illness, waking up everyday to add another frivolous demand to my will. To prove I had desires outside of these sinful ones, to prove I could be good and righteous and all of those things I am no longer concerned with.

These stubborn thoughts and my increasingly difficult-to-deny reality threaten my plastic paradise. Like a serpent, it slithers between the incessant sermons and sinks its fangs deep into the flesh of my rib trying to reach my once-guarded heart. They always instruct you to stay on guard. The devil is lurking in the most unassuming of places. I finally understand what they are afraid of now. Times like this when I sit a little too close to my girl-friend, fingers barely touching, and yet every fiber of my being is on fire. She has no idea what she does to me. The suspiciously quick beating of my heart acts like a ritual drum for my eternal damnation. I nearly choke when I can finally see that my garden is dying. I am the bad apple that spoiled the bunch and because of me what was once lush is now barren, a field filled only with rotten fruit and my own divine deception. Like a budding shepherd, I take my first steps out of the garden hoping to gather the pieces of myself that I've neglected for so long.

This journey is long and treacherous, but it is mine to conquer alone. I don't know when I'll be finished, but I can only hope that the grass really will be greener on the other side. There is safety in numbers, but I find peace in this partial solitude as I climb one hill after another, each seeming smaller than the last. And as the two of us travel along this road, each blur of green no different than the other, my mother finally breaks her temporary vow of silence. "Okay," she says barely above a whisper. Like she's afraid too of what she just said. Afraid of what this means for her and me (but mostly her).

I wonder if she's thinking of all the times she put me in blue instead of pink as a baby. She's probably wondering if there's anything she could have done differently. I could tell her right now that there's not, but I know that's something she'll have to come to terms with on her own.

Nonetheless, okay is all I could pray for. I am grateful for this assurance that she heard me. This reassurance that we'll be alright and that the world will keep spinning on its axis and that I haven't upset the balance of good and evil with my murmured truth. We continue driving and, in the distance, I see the same scenic pastures I always see, still rich and fertile as ever. Everything is the same as it's always been.

—Dallas Knox—

I'm not letting go
   —*Ivy L. James*

my heart has teeth

I bite down and refuse to give up whatever—
          whoever—
                    I love

my heart has nails

I dig in with both hands,
          selfish and greedy

my heart growls

just try to pry me away,
          you bastards,
                    I dare you

my heart is soft with a core of steel

you can't break my grip.
          I'll die before I give up on this—
                    catch me rotting in the searing sun
                    before I go to my knees

—Ivy L. James—

Boy in Blue Jock Strap
—Shane Allison

—Shane Allison—

I am in the minority.

  —*Zoe Harvey-Prioleau*

I won't bow to the white man.

I'll shoot this pretty face.

Before anyone touches me.

I'm thicker than I look.

Blacker than the night.

Guns arranging, guns blazing.

Forced on the ground.

Crying tears, I can't get up.

Please help me momma I'm scared.

Tell my sister I didn't mean it.

I promised Daddy I´d succeed.

Bubba, please I'm sorry.

They got me in cuffs.

I'm singing.

To the lord to take me.

Blood has shuddered from my lips.

My two-toned precious lips.

I'm quivering.

I'm shivering.

I'm mirroring your face.

I'm on the floor

I'm beaten up

bruises on my waist

My love is so sincere

I promise baby I'm here

I swear I'll make it another day

I don't wanna die not yet god, please!

I got a family!

I want a baby!

Let me bless my aunties and my uncles.

I wanna see my grandmama and my granddaddy before the holy bible.

Great horror I face

let me see my brothers and sisters.

Before the days are over.

Please don't make me scream.

Only when the day is through.

I'm finna escape like Harriet man.

— Zoe Harvey-Prioleau —

Underground I'll be on that bus with Rosa.

By your own people Tyre.

I can't breathe said George.

Breonna's momma crying man you took her baby.

On god, I'm finna see Emmett till

and my wrong boy executed George Stinney.

Im sorry babies I know it was wrong of them..

cops won't rot…

But they go in all our hearts.

Bless me with holy matrimony.

Let me have my kids.

Give me a job.

Don't put me underground.

Let me speak.

Let me yell.

Let me see.

Let me be Free…

—Zoe Harvey-Prioleau—

Six years in my twenties
—*Samantha Tucker*

He looked like a dentist, with a bright smile and neat white teeth, but turned out to be a kidney doctor. We got together by mistake and that was six years of my life gone, turned out and filled up. Even as I said yes to his second marriage proposal, I knew I would never marry him. I said yes to buy myself time.

I think what drew me towards him like a boomerang always coming home, was the deep sense of certainty that you felt when you were around him. He made it seem like I could do anything, be anyone.

On our first date he tried to carry my backpack and I refused. I got this, I said. We rode the underground together from Marylebone near my office to Seven Dials, Covent Garden in the direction of 18 inch pizzas, and I noted that his hands looked like a farmers: freckled, strawberry blonde hairs hinted at, squared thumb nails. He was clearly too old for me.

He had a cold bitch of an ex-wife, whose name he called me four times over the course of our relationship, and everytime it happened I was so mad. Once when out running, he turned back to warn me about a fox-hole on the far side of a stile and said '*Fiona*'.

The hole was obscured by bog and bracken, mud and rainwater. There's a good chance I might have tripped right into it if he hadn't said. Fiona was thin and blonde, rode horses for fun and had a terrible relationship with her father. I knew that when she was pregnant with their first child, the smell of apples made her sick. Even apple yoghurt. Once her name was there in the field, muddied into the air, I refused to speak until we got home to the cottage with the blue front door. I tramped onwards with a renewed sense of speed and anger. No-one wants to be someone else's girl. I was me until I wasn't.

But aside from this, he was good at being a boyfriend. Cooked sweetcorn and chilli risotto, made hampers of gifts, took me on lavish trips, always made sure the details were taken care of. I could just show up with a pre-paid ticket to my life. I guess that's why I left, eventually. Being a spectator was strange. Passive. Manageable for a bit, dangerous for too long. I look back and can see myself on the bed as he moved above me, my eyes trained on the ceiling, observing the clutch of bohemian tassels hanging from the lampshade.

One January, I broke my ring-finger while swimming in the sea. I took it as a sign,a reminder, that some things are never meant to be. My engagement ring went back into its box on the lemon carpet, next to the bookcase cubes. We argued about plug adapters and why I didn't want to have sex anymore. Breaking-up felt impossible. I was safe and this was comfortable. How can anyone push away a puppy that refused to leave their side?

Months later, I still received flowers and biscuits and balloons. Back in the cold sea with my now healed, naked fingers, I ducked under, rose to the surface and blew out air. Deciding to go was like exhaling after a very long time.

—*Samantha Tucker*—

Clearance

—James Asava

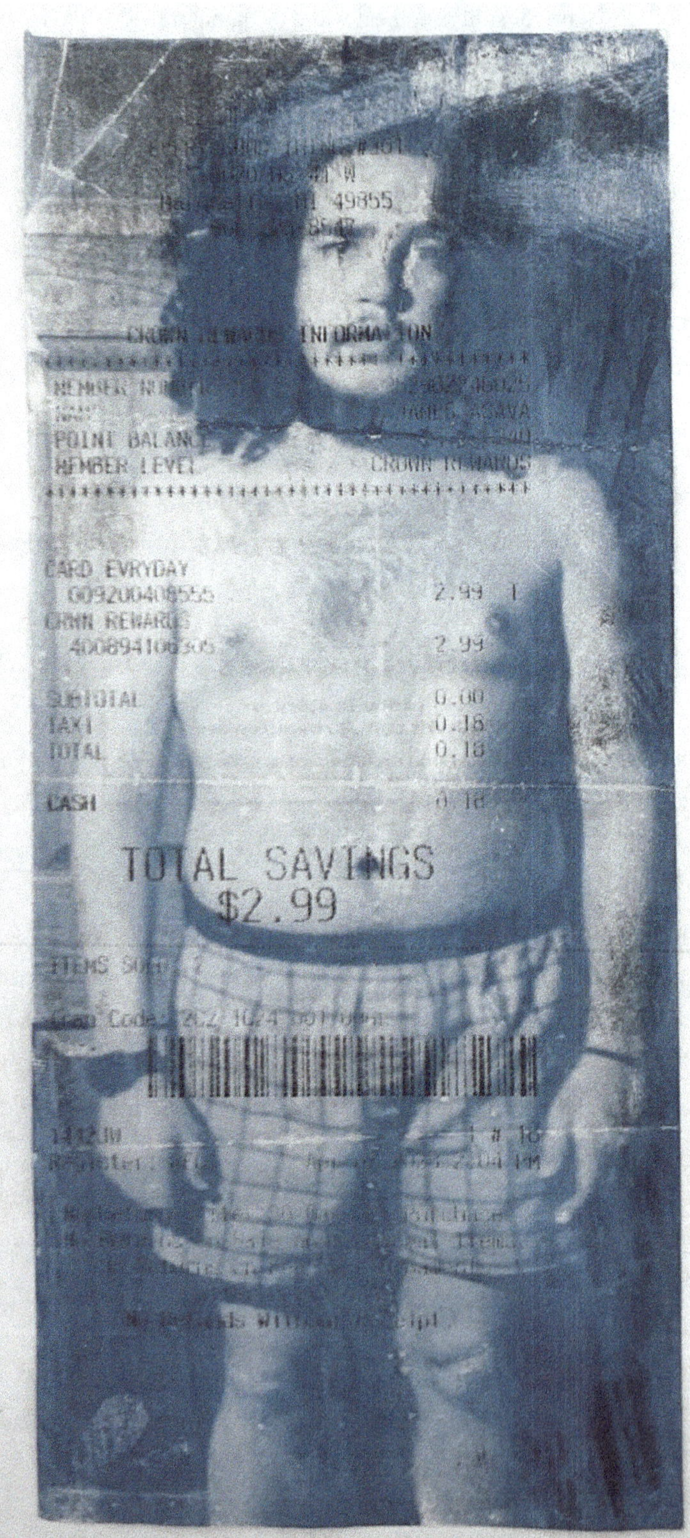

The House on the Hill
   —Carella Keil

The tinfoil from a pack of cigarettes. The Armani watch he's pawned four times. The first key she gave him (a faulty copy, it broke in the lock the day he moved in). The belt with the nickel buckle he swears is turning his treasure-trail green. The angry nest of wire hangers on the closet floor. A half-empty bottle of cologne. A twist-tie wrapped to the size of his fiancé's ring finger. A box of DVDs under the bed. A handful of condoms. All these things, tell her he'll be back. Nothing excites her more than the vial he left on the nightstand this morning.

There's not a lot of sunlight left in this room, the afternoons tilt to shadow. Summers past, she'd spray tangerine perfume on her neck, the insides of her wrists. He'd lift her wrists to his lips, inhale, smile. She wore purple halter-tops and her dark hair in tangled Bedouin braids. She knew there were girls far prettier than her, with fluttery eyelashes and glossed candy-apple lips, but she also knew she had goddess hips, and so he'd never stray far. He liked looking into her eyes, deeper and deeper, until he fell through her and in their blackness, he could sense the wonder of himself.

**Originally published in The Antigonish Review 214*

—Carella Keil—

Tsola
(Tobacco)
  —*Sage Ravenwood*

She saw it all
In the grocery store
Her tree hating neighbors standing in line
        red faced paying in cash – card declined
Through the kitchen screen door
        a woman carrying armloads of fed up
        and done with your son clothes on hangers
Car trunk full of 'this is where we end' belongings
Dumped unceremoniously on a parent's porch
Their son returning to the nest of failed relationships
His poor chihuahua unhomed
        left in the 'what did I do' mixup.
She sees her oversized pup standing at the screen door
        worry creasing his face over the small dog
No one is ever home in the now house of three
Across the street a backhoe gurgles to life
        on a treeless lot growing an RV Camper
Life treading threadbare until you can see
        streets beyond telephone wires no longer
        losing the arm-wrestling battle with branches
In the midst of all this misery a 'bluebird of happiness'
        perches on a wood fence chattering away
She hangs a brand-new bird feeder just in case
The father next door sits on his steps staying put
        in spite of his wife's scorn
Cigarette smoke drifts through her screen door
He's an on again off again smoker
Smoke signaling his son's newfound freedom
        failure in the relationship lotto
She nods acquiesce to this unkindness
No tobacco offering is going to fix suburbia
A blue jay discovers the feeder
But its an offering nonetheless
        to unflesh sorrow

—Sage Ravenwood—

Lit Cigarette Summer
—*Sage Ravenwood*

I wanted a clove cigarette so bad

I could taste it like a dying wish
The hazy subterranean milk skies
Created far more damage than a cigarette drag

lungs sandbagging wildfire

microfine particles slipstreaming veins
Go ahead and finish what you started
Torch my mother's dress, slash her Achilles
She's got nowhere to run

Gray ash the living out of everything
Hide our shame like the reservation dead
God's nothing but a crossdressing Lucifer
standing in the midst of millions
of scorched Earth acreage
Stamping the wild out of anything
not created in his image

I could tolerate the sun's mucus if
in another world Bambi's mom survived
Forest wildings standing in defiance
among burnt umbrage

My pup is shaking in his sleep again

Haven't you been listening
Our extinction is their survival
We kill trees centuries old as if
our time on this planet is nothing
but an illusion

Of all the gods of destruction   which one
gave us the tools behind Abraham's back
Little kids pretending to fix things
with daddy's toolbox

—Sage Ravenwood—

They're calling this the new normal
Ghettoized sky milked of color
I'm only alive for so long, I miss the birds
The days are a blurred Van Gogh

Lack of vibrance is a bad comedian's mic drop

When the smoke mutes autumn
       winter snow falling like ash
No one will see the forest for the trees

or remember like all bad things we tuck away

—Sage Ravenwood—

Gristle

—Isaac Salazar

—Isaac Salazar—

The world is a burning haibun

—Jaimee Boake

We call it wildfire season like it's any other weather, like people aren't responsible for 61% of the burning, like we don't all eventually turn to ash. I think about having to leave on short notice and what I would take. I'm lucky to have a practical partner who would think of practical things like passports. I'd be grabbing the pillow made from his grandpa's shirt, soft as a funeral hymn. The blankets crocheted by grandma despite aching hands. Recipes collected from family. Well-loved books and our wedding album. The first outfit our baby ever wore. The bag of pennies leftover from wishing; we may need more miracles. The sweater of yours I like to wear, will wrap myself in it while the world fades.

We ▮▮▮ wildfire ▮▮▮▮▮▮▮▮▮▮▮▮▮▮▮ people ▮▮▮▮▮▮▮▮▮▮▮▮ burning, like we don't all
eventually turn to ash ▮▮▮▮▮▮▮▮▮▮▮▮▮ take ▮▮▮▮▮▮
▮▮▮▮▮ things ▮▮▮▮▮▮▮▮▮ made ▮▮▮▮▮▮ soft ▮
▮▮▮ by ▮▮▮▮ aching hands ▮▮▮▮▮▮▮▮▮▮
▮▮▮▮▮▮▮▮▮▮▮▮ leftover ▮▮▮▮▮▮
miracles ▮▮▮▮▮▮▮▮▮▮▮ while the world fades.

We ▮▮ wildfire ▮▮▮▮▮▮▮▮▮ people ▮▮▮▮▮▮▮ burning, ▮▮▮▮
▮▮▮▮ to ash ▮▮▮▮▮▮▮▮▮▮▮▮▮
▮▮▮▮▮▮▮▮▮▮▮ made ▮▮▮▮ soft ▮
▮▮▮ by ▮▮▮ aching ▮▮▮▮▮▮
▮▮▮▮▮▮▮▮▮▮▮▮▮▮
miracles ▮▮▮▮▮▮▮▮

13 Reasons Why Not

—Jaimee Boake

i. Because the trees are budding beneath a spring breeze like fresh breath. Because the birds are back

ii. home; a hummingbird just this morning at the window, wings swift

iii. as it sought sweet things in the garden, sucked nectar from flowers; what a hope filled fluttering,

iv. room for all that lightness in hollow bones. A body made for soaring.

v. The only bird capable of backwards flight, of choosing any direction

vi. guided by their memories of a place. Perhaps, this is the way

vii. we carve space for ourselves in wide wild.

viii. Supposedly it's good luck to see one, and so I thought of you,

ix. you who also sees the world in colours others can't,

x. whose heart beats an impossible rhythm.

xi. Though the bird is strong enough to be solitary,

xii. a flock can be called a bouquet, a glittering, a shimmer, a tune; such brightness.

xiii. You can rename yourself something beautiful too like safe, like seen, like a song.

—Jaimee Boake—

Disappearing Acts

—Frankie Concepcion

Act I.

We knew it would happen one way or another. We'd heard the stories before. Grown up with them– they fortified our bones. As girls, our mothers had fed us warnings: how not to deserve it, how not to invite it, how to be smarter and tougher and faster than those who did. How no matter how we prepared, some of us were just unlucky. In the end, they said, it was inevitable– some are just bound to disappear.

When it started, you barely noticed. Amena, on her way home from the market, disappeared on her way to the shuttle that would have taken her home. A schoolteacher's daughter, she was gone for a week before her family had gathered enough money to convince the police to try and find her.

Then there was Thea, known for her vanishing acts– for missing curfew and cutting class. One night, she missed the dormitory roll call and did not return. The next morning the school called her parents, who then cut their vacation short and flew back to the city to find her. Not wanting to make a fuss, they hired a private investigator instead of bribing the police. But when asked to provide leads, they realized that their daughter had been a stranger to them for years.

Soon after went the twins with the Ivy league dreams, after a test that brought them both to tears. Rina and Sally at a sleepover. Kumiko, the class president, Jessie with the oily hair, Aretha who got A's in every class but gym. Girls you thought no one would want and girls who seemed to be asking for it. We disappeared from school, from parties, from the mall, from our own beds. We disappeared one by one, or in pairs, our absences noticed immediately, noticed not at all. Until one day you woke up and found no more of us.

Act II.

You started by asking all the obvious questions. Did we have secrets? Any hidden desires? Were there reasons we might have had for leaving? (Though no one asked: what reason did we have to stay?) What were we wearing? Who were we with, and what had we done to make them jealous? To make them angry? To make them want us for themselves?

In other words: what had we done to deserve this?

Pictures of us began to appear at the grocery store and the town hall; they papered the walls of our schools. Airbrushed faces, itchy dresses, and hairstyles we would never wear unless forced. Obsolete from the beginning.

Some of you went straight to mourning. In the Church where you taught us about heaven and hell, you held a vigil in our honor. You recounted all the things you loved best about us, forgave us for our trespasses (for all we had done and failed to do). At night you dreamed about us, and in your dreams we said *thank you,* said *I'm sorry,* said *I'm at peace.* But in the morning we were still gone.

Still, some of you looked for someone else to blame. You read our diaries, found our hiding places, all the things we'd been taught to keep secret. In one notebook, a picture of the boy we once thought we might have loved. For a moment, you turned your suspicious eyes on him. But soon he was deemed too promising for punishment, and it was easier instead to put the blame on us and on our hearts, our new and fickle hearts, on wanting so badly to know how it felt to break them.

You searched for us. Stripped of our bodies, left only with our desires, we became unrecognizable to you. You tried to lay the thread of us out from beginning to end, searching for that first knot –too late, too late– for the place where it all began to tangle together.

But you will never find us. We were already lost to you.

Act III.

It is decided that what happened to us is what always happens: that our disappearance was against our will. Why, after all, would we want to leave? Why forgo all that the world has to offer? We who had been given so much and yet asked for so little. We who knew small, who knew silent, who knew a hundred ways to swallow our want and to say yes to the things we didn't. We would have been easy prey, you say. Our own worst enemies.

Where are we?

Would it give you peace to know? Would knowing quell your rage, or stifle your suspicions? Would we live on in your memories rose-tinted, or would we be the stuff of nightmares?

Would you rescue us? Would you keep us hidden, keep us safe forever?

In your dreams are we perfect? Do we make you proud? Do you feed us cake, give us away, fulfill all the long-awaited birthdays and graduations and weddings that once lived so clearly in your mind?

Do we look happy? Do you call us saints? Do you dream us living, or is it easier to believe we are dead?

Where are we?

If we told you already, would you remember? Or would we be all smiles and no voice, all skin and no soul– we who you have already forgotten?

Where are we?

We are taken. We are hiding. We are gone, and yet we are still with you. We are six feet under, locked in a basement, luring children into our candy house. We are underwater mermaid-tailed, we are hitchhiking to Vegas. We are cutting our hair. We are turning frogs into princes, hair into gold, memories into books and movies and art– priceless. We are living our wildest dreams. We are living yours. We are beyond your imagination.

—Frankie Concepcion—

The Call To Be Queer
—Ell Cee

into puddles

   —Nayt Rundquist

Takk

It's a slow process, dissolving into a thunderstorm. A transcendent, sensuous one. Peels you apart, layer by layer. Unmakes me to my nothingness. Cleanses quarks and double helixes, spinning out into everything.

Glósóli

Usually, it's Sigur Rós wandering those puddle-sodden roads with me. My ears drinking in the Hopelandish they can't translate. But my spirit understands hopping bootless into puddles—resonates with star elves and blue skies—dissolves into lilting, untitled, parenthetical instrumentals. Air smells earthy electric—a deep vibrant green—chilly and invigorating.

Hoppípolla

Worship for my teenaged soul. A path outward. An escape from the body that never quite fits, the belonging that never roosts for long.

Með blóðnasir

Each raindrop permeates my skin—slices painless through to bone. And as they splash back away, mingling in puddles and soaking dirt roads to mud, they pull me away. One cell at a time.

Sé lest

My musculature ripples off into fat grey clouds, rolls across the sky. Loose gravel beneath my soles a gentle tether to now, pinpricks of delightful, warm pain mirroring the exhilarating splatter from above.

Sæglópur

Nerves unspool, untangle, reach out to dance along lightning strikes flickering through cumulonimbus. Every blade of grass weighed down and waving in winds. Every ant trapped by surface tension, hiding under stones, leaf-rafting down gutters. Each tree, branches lacing flirty fingers with negative ions, trunks swaying and groaning ecstatic, roots singing the song of this storm deep, deep, deep underground.

Mílanó

am egodead. but molecules and mysteries. winds and flashes and rumbles through dark greyblue skies. senseless, meandering. under- over- through- omni- super- quantum-. between and within. contained and containing. -neath -all -out -present -position -entangled.

Gong

Heartbeat is every peal of thunder rolling across the landscape, escaping beyond even the storm's nebulous bounds. As itandI wander, drift along fronts, aimless but headed for some destination, even if that's just where we fall apart again, expending all our energy and dissipate back into ether again. My clouds pull apart, white cotton-candy fluff and sky pushes back to cerulean and sun shines through me, hauling warm along with it.

Andvari

Still and serenity permeate. Petrichor draws disparate home. The specks of eternity that remember they were me—or imagine they were—gravitate, coalesce, corporealize.

—Nayt Rundquist—

Svo hljótt

Sense returns to body as it rebuilds. Molecules click back into place, Lego bricks of my entirety. Vision unclouds, clearing after rubbing your eyes too hard, relief after too long without eating, without drinking. The air tastes of clay, smells of the song of greenery giving thanks. Gooseflesh dances along arms, along legs. Shirt clings drenched, second skin protecting the first. Shorts are sodden, heavy, anchoring. Residual raindrops drip from hair past eyes—a microcosm of (every)where I'd gone.

Heysátan

I'm in a field between a church and a playground. I'm on a road orbiting an elementary school. I think Kroger is several streets that way. Maybe the high school is over there. I'm triangulating between three friends' houses, guessing at landmarks.

Silence

Press play again. Start the long wander home.

—Nayt Rundquist—

GEN Z POEM ABOUT THE THESIS OF SURVIVAL
—Mubarak Said TPC XII

History made me remember that I lost my pride the day I was born &my father loved his garden

in the same way, he loved praying, so he named our carrot, garden egg &rosary bead.

This is how I know I can't always fly like a bird, I have to first grow wings. Some days I wake to the sound of

the wind, sweeping away a tattered kiss. My eardrum is sensitive to a romantic poem which means:

I know all it takes to feed, raise and lull a heart. This is the thesis of survival: My hands are my room, my pen, and my bed.

This is how the wind sweeps a bare land, giving it another name; a sea, a valley.

I read the book of life, I read poetry and I see the wavering of my days amidst nights.

The shadows of my words appear like snow saturating my sweat.

Anything that has taken a new face dies by sleeping away from home

instead of learning we're born to reshape the map.

— Mubarak Said TPC XII—

The Power of Risk

—Sara Collie

—Sara Collie—

MOTHER RETURNED

—Angeleen Rohda

My name is Angeleen, which means messenger of God. But this messenger couldn't forewarn me of the pain of losing my mothers.

As an infant I lost my biological mother, her name is Ellaura, which means wisdom. This loss created a hole that went largely unacknowledged by myself and the world at large until I would be a middle-aged woman, finally getting validation of all the ways it affected me and reflected on me.

At 13-years-old I lost my adopted mother, her name is Wennet, it means blessed. She was the only woman I had ever called mom. She was the known figure to which I clung to keep from falling down the seemingly bottomless cavity of the unknown. It seemed all my childhood fears came to pass when she passed. The nights I would fall asleep crying because I could not imagine a life without her seemed prophetic.

At 25-years-old I met Ellaura, while the gape that was left years before has never been repaired fully, she was the connection I always felt was missing. The square door that led to knowing myself. After a lifetime of feeling like a puzzle piece that was put in the wrong box by an incompetent employee, I had found my box. Years spent imagining the space she would take up was now known. Still, I feared she would leave me again, and that fear filled me with snakes coiling and uncoiling under my skin, changing the look of me.

Losing Ellaura at birth, gaining Wennet in infancy, losing Wennet as a teenager, gaining Ellaura as a young adult, I saw the next part of the pattern and it was not pleasing.

I vowed to take nothing for granted and I began to unravel the complexity of Ellaura's motherhood and inner thoughts, which informed my own. Things I will never have the opportunity to do with Wennet, instead, she is frozen at 42 in my mind. When I turned 42 myself, I was told my intended birth name was Yetunde, which means mother returned. And I thought of my lost mothers, and I cried.

This informed me too and again; my shape began to change.

I close my eyes and imagine a world where my two mothers would meet. This ever-evolving daydream takes on various forms, morphing with my mood and how honest I want to be. But my favorite construction is where they will hug and cry. Proud of who I have become, knowing the part they played and holding gratitude to the other for the parts they didn't.

Wennet and Ellaura, their combined silhouette together only in my mind.

—Angeleen Rohda—

This Mother's Day Iresha spoke of healing our mothers' wounds, that before they were our mothers, they were broken by being someone else's daughter. That they mothered only to the extent that they were mothered. And now, we can make a conscious decision to choose healing. To heal our mothers' wounds.

And my mind returns to Ellaura and Wennet and the wounds I know and those I never will.
That same day my daughter, Lilah, which means night beauty, forwarded me a message saying: "I wish I could go back and mother my mother and give her all the love she deserved but didn't receive. That's how I feel about you." She texted me. And again, I wept. Kaya told me tears are healing and to not be so quick to wipe them away.

I was taught to cry by the wounds left in my own mothers and the wounds my mothers left in me. All those empty caverns begging to be filled. While I cry, I have never seen Wennet cry, though her wounds were many. "I cry for her too," I think.

I again return to that special imaginary image where my two mothers are together at once, their bodies side by side create a new outline that is more real in its impression on me than in the space that life has allowed. This time though, I stand next to them, the silhouette adjusts making a new shape.

—Angeleen Rohda—

It's In Our Hands
   —Sarah Blakely

We stood, one with the oak trees out in the wild,
overlooking the forest, inhaling pollen.

The hike leader gave us peanut M&Ms,
imperfect miniature globes in our young hands.

We learned about the Earth's crust that day,
sweet chocolate, it disappeared rapidly.

—Sarah Blakely—

Wanderlust
  —*Emma Geller*

—*Emma Geller*—

Past the Crickets in the Tall Summer Grass
—J.D. Isip

San Pedro, 1992

We are out of breath, soaked in sweat and dew. Anthony can't stop laughing, the moon spotlights his white chest. We all shed our shirts and shorts, Cody's letterman jacket he's only had for months. All lost in the sand and the grass, somewhere between the Korean Friendship Bell and the highway where we are waiting for Cody's mom, down to our underwear. Before we could ring it, there was rustling behind us. Then the blinding skunk smell in our mouths and throats and eyes. We tried our best to outrun it. Tried our best to keep down the pregame wine coolers and cheese sticks. I wanted to turn back for the jacket; I spent three months' pay on it. Even though I knew it was ruined. Cody turned me around, pointed at Anthony in the moonlight, twirled his finger to his temple, *I think he's lost it!* When his mom pulled up, she said, "I could see all of you naked a mile away" and she kept saying, "None of you better throw up in my car." I don't know how all of us, nearly men, squeezed into the tub, when and how the cans of tomato sauce got opened or poured on us. I just remember rinsing it all off, the skunk, the tomato bits, the shards of grass. Anthony and Cody, towels around their waists, recounting the bell, the skunk, and the shoes we shucked. Something else was missing. The graduation ring Cody bought me, just a little loose on my finger. *Where did it slip off?* I'd had it for such a short time. Every now and then I think of going back to find it. They say a bell can't be unrung, but what if you never got to ring it?

—J.D. Isip—

Mud

  —Seth Kronick

rotten, murky mud
with oodles of oozing bubbles
and spirts of oily dirt
rearing patches of reeking, yellowed sludge
with greenish shoots sticking out
where itty-bitties and creepy-crawlies dwell
near the long, orange tree specks of gnat

—Seth Kronick—

Snail Lady

—Auguste Fallon

DEEP IN THE
NORTH BERKELEY
HILLS
LIVES THE SNAIL
LADY.
ONCE A BARISTA,
NOW HERSELF.
SHE CLIMBS AND
CRAWLS UP TREES,
FEARS SODIUM AND
MUNCHES ON
HALLUCINOGENS.

LOVE YOURSELF
FOR NO ONE ELSE
WILL,
BE YOURSELF
BECAUSE NO ONE
ELSE CAN.
ENJOY YOURSELF
FOR WITHOUT
THAT THE WORLD
IS BLAND.

—Auguste Fallon—

Three Swims to the Island

—Zary Fekete

I pull the car into the driveway. It's my wife's mother's house. We're here for the summer…my wife and two boys. Her mother is having a party for the people who work for her.

We ring the doorbell and her mother opens the door.

"Come in, then." she says. She's been drinking some. She puts a spatula in my hand and tells me to help with the grill out back. My wife tells me she can handle the bags. I walk out back and start flipping burgers.

It's a hot evening. The grill makes where I stand hotter. Each time I flip a burger my skin feels singed. Sweat gathers by my temples and under my arms.

It's a big party. There are people indoors and out. Most people are drinking. There are bottles and cans everywhere.

It's been 18 months since I've smelled people drinking. My wife is upstairs with the boys. I flip the burgers, thinking. The downstairs fridge is just inside the door from the grill. I slip inside, looking for a bathroom.

***

We've been here a week now. I'm out back with my younger son. We're looking at the lake. The air is heavy and thick. We're both wearing our swim suits. We come up with a game…which one of us can jump out farther.

We play a few rounds. Each time I climb out I brush away mosquitos. One of them finds a place on my ankle. I scratch at the bite.

After we jump for awhile I squint out at the lake. There's a small island out in the cove.

"Let's swim out there," I say to my son. He shields his eyes and looks out.

"Isn't that too far?"

"No, it'll be fine," I say, with a grin.

We start swimming. The water is warm like a bath. Some of it sloshes sloppily into my mouth.

We get to the island and sit in the shallow water. Small waves sweep up against our wet suits, lifting the fabric up and down. I talk to my son about something.

We swim back. That night when everyone is asleep I go downstairs.

***

Another week. My younger son and I are out at the water again. The mosquito bites on my legs are itching me, and I scratch them hard even though someone told me that doesn't help. My son and I play a few rounds of the jumping game.

"Island again?" I say. I can tell he doesn't want to. It's actually pretty far. He doesn't say no, because he likes doing something with me.

—Zary Fekete—

We jump into the water and start to pull. The water is warmer. Someone said it doesn't fully cool down here until November.

We get to the island and sit in the shallows again. The water laps against my legs while I absently brush at the mosquitos. We don't talk much.

***

We've been here a month. My body is slack and sallow, especially in the evenings. I don't know where my family is today. I put on my swimming suit and go down to the lake.

The water is dead still. The sun on it hurts my eyes. I squint out at the island. I jump up and down a few times. I run and jump into the water and let my body sink all the way down to the muck below. The water down here is cool. I let my feet sink into the slime at the bottom of the lake. It's easier to stay down here, away from the hot sun and light.

I float back up to the warm surface. I get out and jump several more times, each time feeling my skin in my face move with the air, loose and lank. I feel the liquid in my stomach slosh every time I jump. Finally, exhausted, I stand by the shore, my feet covered with mosquitos, more and more arriving all the time.

I jump in one more time and start to swim toward the island alone.

—Zary Fekete—

Swamp Song

—Liv Merritt

The air is thick and heavy
Eyes are heavy-lidded
Spanish moss reaches for me
As the bayou straggles along

Everything is buzzing
Lulling me with swamp song
The cypresses are singing
As an ibis drifts overhead

There is rot in my lungs
And cotton in my mouth
I cannot move my tongue
Porch swing creaks under me

Cypress knees rise out
Of brackish, crawling water
Still your fevered doubt
Feel the heat within

—Liv Merritt—

The Queen's Garden
   —*Jenna Johnson*

Pencil, Felt Pen, Alcohol Markers
8"x10"

The Golden Boy

—Franchon Whitby

My dog's big snout steams up random parcels of dry December grass as we walk up our road. The late afternoon light appears to slant heavier, more golden, across the houses on the other side of the street. As we walk, a vivid canopy of crisping oak leaves draws my eyes up. A sole raven caws at me as I pass under him, his black form such a stunning contrast against the russet and golds that he believed hid him so well.

At the end of my walk, I notice a woman across the street. She is standing at the top of her steep driveway, the back door of her SUV waiting, open. I have seen this woman many times over the years, but I don't know her name. She has two young children. I recall hearing their infant wailings during the "witching hour" when she'd leave their front door open on hot summer evenings as I walked another big dog, nearly identical to the one I'm walking now.

A little boy is by her side. He is older now. By my guess, 7 years old. He is no longer a baby, or a toddler. He is a little person about to go somewhere with his mom. He is bouncy on his feet. Maybe testing out new Christmas sneakers for the first time. He is about to climb up into the back seat when she suddenly stops him. She gently pulls him by the sleeve of his micro down jacket, then reaches for his other arm and pivots him to face her. He is suddenly still like a little soldier boy. He tilts his head way back and looks up at his mother. His entire face is bathed in heavy golden light. I can't hear her, but I am a mother of a former little boy and I know she is just taking a moment for herself. To stop time. To check in with him. To take a quick Polaroid with her eyes of this fleeting version of her little boy standing in the beautiful golden light at the top of their driveway on a cool December afternoon. She reaches down, zips up his jacket and retrieves a small comb from somewhere that I can't see. I think how formal and unusual it is to see a mother use a comb, when fingers are the expected tool, especially outside. She lovingly glides the comb through her son's soft brown hair. First the left side, then the right. She takes his still upturned face into her hands and kisses him softy on the right cheek. Though I can't see it, I know he smiles at her right before he turns and bounds into the backseat. She closes his door softly. She gets into the driver's seat. I know she looks over her shoulder to make sure her son has successfully clicked himself into his booster seat before she begins to back down the steep driveway.

She slowly reverses into the road, then heads west up our street. She is content. The radio, a quiet backdrop, enshrouds them. In the backseat, her precious son's cheek is still moist with her kiss and the golden afternoon light chases the roof of their car.

—Franchon Whitby—

Down by the River, You Climb Trees in the Dark
  —Karen Keefe

I know why
but you won't tell the ER docs.

Tears dissolve streaks of mud on your cheek.
I turn off the bright cubicle light
reach under the warmed blanket to hold your hand.

Sunset. You snuck out of the house
to lie in the wet muck and watch worms.
Then you climbed a tree to look for our mother.

Did you still see the shape of her
by the back door?
Did you hear her whistle when you fell?

For weeks at bedtime, you tell me
about watching dew worms.
You think
any worms will be gentle
as they move in and out
around and through the empty
eye sockets of people buried
underground
like our mother is.

They slide across the bone
like a caress
leaving a trail of shining slime
it could be fluorescent.

You wonder how worm slime feels
is it like tears sliding down your cheek?

Can you be right?
Will the ground creatures
hold our mother
gently
caress her
and place their heads
against
what was once
her cheek?

—Karen Keefe—

The Fawn
  —*Catherine Broadwall*

—*Catherine Broadwall*—

ON FINDING A DEAD DEER IN MY BACKYARD
  —Nolo Segundo

I saw them a few weeks ago. My wife called me, something urgent—
so I left the computer and went to see what so excited her.

Three deer, 3 young deer meandering around our ¼ acre backyard.
They look thin, she said—I agreed
(not saying it was not a good sign with winter coming near).

We enjoyed watching them through our plate glass door, their
casual grace, that elegance of walk deer have when unafraid.
They were special, even more than the occasional cardinal
alighting in our yard like a breathing ruby with wings—so
we stayed as still as possible. I told her that deer can only see
what moves, so we held ourselves tight like insensate statues.

Two of these white-tailed beauties grazed daintily on the ground
but the third was drawn to our giant holly tree, resplendent
with its myriad red berries, like necklaces thrown capricious.
I was concerned—something alarming about even deer drawn
like the proverbial moth—safe, I wondered, for deer or tree?

The triplets soon left our yard, as casually as they had come,
and a week went by—then one day a single deer came back.
I say back because she went straight for the holly tree, and
I banged on the plate glass door and yelled as fierce as an
old man can yell to scare off the now unwanted intruder, for
something told me the holly tree would be death to the deer.

She fled, but the next day came back again, again alone, and
again with eyes only for that tree, an Eve that could not say
no to the forbidden fruit—or berries or leaves it appears.
Again I chased her away, and for a few days saw no return.

Then one brisk morning our neighbor called—he saw what
we could not see in the deep green thickness of that holly tree.
The doe lay sleeping under its canopy (so death always seems
with animals, unlike a human corpse where something is gone),
killed it seemed by berries or the leaves of the innocent tree.

—Nolo Segundo—

I called my township—they said, put the carcass by the street,
we'll send someone to pick it up—but I couldn't, or wouldn't.
Not just because I walk with a cane, and am old and unsure
how such a moving would be done—no, no, it was more—
when I saw the deer lying sheltered beneath the tree it loved,
the tree it died for, it seemed a sacred place, consecrated—
and I could not bring myself to violate nature's holy ground.

Fortunately I have a neighbor who is not sentimental, and he
dragged the dead doe roughly to the curb, and I knew, by
its pungent unearthly smell of death, it was the only answer.

—Nolo Segundo—

Body Speak

—*Annaliese Jakimides*

The drive to live :: today in the present :: is a new combustion, a lens, a viewpoint filtered through a rough draft of a life. The interludes or interstices of what I used to call time before you moved into another space of disembodied particulars.

An ether of soft flame, a smoke of time capsule.

You off to the incinerator. Me on the bus home to receive the box of you from the U.S. Postal Service, the deliverer of the dead. I held onto my mother for decades, my son for a year, and you only long enough for the arrival of the glitter of sunlight on the Penobscot after the day of the blinded rain and the impossible full-sky, top-to-bottom, ridge-to-ridge rainbow, the walkup gallery with the scissored paper boxes made of washi or tengu, maybe kozo or ogura, cascading from the ceiling :: a slip of steep steps to the roof and the clouds :: the crackle of voices :: the blistering silence :: the impossible bridge of colors :: violet, indigo, flickering russet flitting in the breeze :: my hand stilled on the spotless surface of a worn pine table :: narrow shelves of books :: framed maps :: a subtle portrait of two not so subtle toddler girls :: voices a version of an echo around the corner :: laughter :: speckled phrases of beautiful, sometimes unusual, words :: a random *fuck*

Can't stay, too many, too much, too soon.

I drive into the rainbow.

I'm newly tired. And so perhaps. But not. Such clarity. Despite.

Under my tongue, a sequin of rain pools now each night, harvesting what most people think must be the specter of heartbreak or heartloss, heartache, something heart-indefinable-but-painful in body speak but body speak is no longer my chosen language: heart, not the organ or the metaphor, only the container… of all this presence.

On tomorrow's today, rising before sunbreak, at the top of some random perfumed bluff, I'll pick silk threads and crimson flowers, fresh bread, lavender and cod, feel your lips moist on my right shoulder.

—*Annaliese Jakimides*—

Sounding Home

—Annaliese Jakimides

I've been coming again to the park that crosses over the Kenduskeag River downtown, joining Franklin and Central Streets, to stand in one spot and close my eyes. I'm fully aware of what surrounds me, the red brick building that hugs the south side of the park, the yews, the one ancient rhododendron bush, the yarrow. Workers on lunch break often sit on the wooden and stone benches; people stroll through; pigeons congregate. From the opening onto Central, I can always see through the huge panel of windows into the cavernous belly of the Bagel Shop, now called Bagel Central. I'm slow to make name changes—and honestly if you change how you called yourself when we met I will internally stumble for years, maybe forever. Judy became Judith. Sheba forfeited her Black Muslim days and reverted back to Patricia and the Catholics. In my head I translate their naming every time.

I can see the front of the tiny Friar's Bakehouse, run by two monks in brown robes who don't ever seem to be real monks to me, although they are divinely kind and open, have an altar in the upstairs loft with Mary and Jesus, a crucifix, plastic flowers, and come in at three in the morning to bake the daily bread and soup for the people who will eat at the community-supper-size tables.

Today I'm not headed there for lunch or to anywhere else. My goal is to be exactly where I am—in the park—doing what I'm doing—standing with my eyes closed. I have come here a number of times to do this, but usually it begins to feel like an effort, a weight, something I can't tolerate anymore and cast off. It only takes a few minutes for me to get twitchy. Every time, I snap my eyes open and am relieved that everything in the solid universe is as it was when I let it go.

I know that this is not the same as being blind. Light leaks through, and I have the power to return to the visual world. I know all that, but I've been showing up like this for weeks now. Not for long. I'm not misleading myself, but there is a kind of relearning myself that settles into my body.

A few years ago, I stole a public garden patch in this very park I'm practicing blindness and patience in right now. Neglected, overgrown, bookended by a spirea bush and a clump of iris, this garden gives me a place to go, something to keep alive. By the time I had left my forty acres, my gardens—gardens that in the beginning years were all sustenance crops of carrots and lettuce, potatoes, cucumbers, succulent sweet peas—had evolved into landscapes of peonies, iris, lush midnight-blue delphiniums, raging-orange coreopsis.

When I came to this small city, I thought I was over all that dirt under the nails, the hauling and digging, the bending, the watering. Until walking through the little park, I found myself squatting down to clean out some broken stems, a cigarette butt, many cigarette butts. The sun was warm on the back of my neck: a familiar sensation, one I had no recognition of missing until that moment. I've been coming here week after week, spring through fall, ever since. Now when I come, I don't always garden. Sometimes I just stand, balance, unbalance, close my eyes, open them, grateful once again every time that the world has not shifted off its axis.

The first time I stood like this, I was surprised at how quickly I lost my balance, and moved over to feel the stone wall. I didn't need to hold on. Even the back of a hand was good enough. Just a sense of contact between me and something. With practice, that something can now be less stable, like the drooping branch of a scrawny willow, and I can last for more than a few minutes without that painful longing to reenter the world that comes from trying to sort out all the sounds and their directions that demand my attention and prevent me from climbing up into my head.

I never knew I was such a head-climber, a thinker, perhaps even someone who could walk through or by without noticing until I began this practice. It's possible I'm a version of my gone son, who could have walked over a bleeding person, stopped, thought the whole scenario was interesting, and then walked on. If I noticed—and that's the "if" I sense now—I would definitely have stopped, helped, empathized, done something, felt everything.

Today I feel the sun, the heat, the attachment, the loss, my heart galumphing in my chest, straining against the tank top under my jersey. I have no branch within hand's grasp. I stand, light glowing through my closed lids. Lifted up from the canal, pigeons flutter somewhere near my feet, settling on the brick walkway, pecking, likely, at the crumbs of someone's sandwich. Distance is clearer to me now. Time passes—not hours, but many minutes, I'm sure. And I wait. I stand. I balance. I am. Here. Waiting.

>>>

Minutes slip off the clock face. Ooze away. Until every clock—every single one—stops. And all of the calendars disappear.

—Annaliese Jakimides—

The Tod
 —*Michael Putorti*

 —*Michael Putorti—*

Scraps

—Tiffany Overby

Lick me clean, suck
my meat from my bones.

Savor later,
this moment when the long
day is finished
and you lay limp,
and alone.

Flare your nostrils,
with erotic air, knowing
I knew what I was doing.

—*Jillian Clasky*

The first and last time I went hiking,

I was fifteen and hollow and nearly too weak to drag my own body along. On the bus ride, my thighs, thick with sweat, clung to the vinyl upholstery beneath them. When we reached Tobermory, I cleaved my skin from the seat, filed out the door into hot July air, scuffed my soles against dirt. The limestone crag stood firm and ancient underfoot as I trekked from campsite to cliffside. Below me: Georgian Bay, frigid even in the dead of summer, its cold sting turning stale air fresh again. With my toes on the boundary between earth and space, I felt fragile and cavernous enough to fly. The edges of the world began to blur, smudged as if scribbled by a child. I read once, years later, in the hot static of a night without sleep, that the existentialists ascribe the urge to leap from such heights not to suicidality but to the all-consuming anxiety of individual will. Sometimes I wonder if I've ever made a choice: if I ran that summer of my own volition and not just because my bones had grown restless and I knew I could not refuse to follow where they took me. Sometimes I wonder whether I could have split time in two and followed each path to its inevitable conclusion. Instead I let the low hum of the wind dampen the voices around me and splayed my fingers across my chest: a cage over a cage, or rather a cage within a cage; concentric cages, each containing the other. I curled my thumb inward, pressed a crescent into the skin above my rib. This mark would fade in minutes, like a handprint in concrete insistent on its permanence even as the weather wears it down, fingertips stretched across a fault line in the sidewalk as if reaching and failing to bridge two worlds. I was reaching for something even then; what it was I still can't tell. All I know is that the water surged around me, threatened to trawl my future body into its current, and that on the bus ride home I felt not distance but a suffocating proximity to everyone I'd ever been, even as three hundred kilometers of highway spilled open in front of me.

—*Jillian Clasky*—

Apex
—Michael Putorti

—Michael Putorti—

Excerpt from *Cry Wolf*

—Tawnya Torres

Starlings ebb and flow over the horizon, now turning a fresh shade of coral with layers of lavender, and butter. They move mechanically like robot toys rather than lively creatures. The birds create serpentine monsters, dragons and snakes, slithering to their goodbye.

"Almost ready," says Trey, adjusting his camera, looking through the lens then at real life, and again through his own vision. He wants to make it perfect.

"What are we doing again?" asks Missy.

"He's going to take photos of us," I say and put my hand in the curtain of ivy hanging in front of me. Trey has us stand by a hawthorn tree, ripe with spring and full of clusters of white blossoms. It's golden hour, the sun remaining in the sky soon to be gone without a trace.

"Why do people have photos?" she asks.

"To remember important moments."

Trey moves the camera two feet to the left, then a foot to the right, settling somewhere in the middle. His equipment is professional but his attire is casual, like him. A fuchsia and yellow windbreaker, black pants, and white sneakers.

"Alright, I'm all set," says Trey with a lopsided grin. He looks at us and I feel my neck grow warm and my face flushes.

"What should we do?" asks Missy and Trey approaches, hands itching to make beautiful things.

"Missy, you stand here," says Trey, posing her in the glimmer of sun. "And Shane, I want you to stand here and face each other."

I'm not one for vanity and my scalp begins to sweat. Trey pulls me closer to Missy and we stand intimately close. I can have sex with someone easier than engaging in a staring contest. It's something I struggle with, being seen. Right now Missy is looking up at me, eyelashes casting butterfly shadows on her face.

"Am I doing it right?" asks Missy and Trey nods.

"You're a great model. Now, put your hand on his chest and your other on his shoulder," Trey instructs and Missy follows. "Shane, put your hand here," he says, putting my hand facing the camera on her hip.

"Like this?" I ask, unsure of how good of a model I am.

"Don't move," says Trey as he runs back to his camera, white sneakers connect with the grass in my peripheral, but I'm looking right at Missy.

The foreign eye color, honey amber and gold, is it prevalent somewhere else in the world? Her skin is fair and her hair was more red than brown. Is she European? Do they have eyes fit to see in the dark in Russia or Australia?

I didn't find any bruises on her when I brought her home the day I shot her. Other than the damage I caused she was healthy and well-fed. No marks around her wrists or ankles. Whatever life she lived before me, please don't let it be cruel. I imagine she was an adventurer, a seeker, a nature enthusiast or simply a nudist. Anything but a captive, a slave, a victim.

"Is this an important moment?" asks Missy.

In my old phones and computer I have photos of me and my ex-girlfriends. I can't bring myself to delete them, though I don't look at them. There's times where I think of them but I opt to not click on their file. Important, or not all. Either way I can't stand to forget, even if it's bad.

—Tawnya Torres—

"It is," I say and as the sun blinds me as it brushes through the ivy in the tree. Missy presses into me as she surprises me with a kiss and I hear the camera click several times.

The heat from her kiss and the shimmering sun melt away a portion of resentment, opening me up to the luck I've had. My childhood was turbulent but non-violent. I've met a lot of bad people but also great people like Trey and Walter and John and Travis. Before I met Missy I was so focused on avoiding my negative feelings, I didn't take in anything good happening around me.

No apology can fix my past. Nothing but forgiveness can rescue me from the hate I have for my mom and for myself. It all seems insignificant now. Now I know why. Every moment leads us closer to where we are supposed to be. I was meant to be here, in Oregon, with her. The mistakes I made, the decisions I made but also didn't make, lead me here to this moment where I can let go as I hold on to this girl with an unknown past.

"Perfect," says Trey as he steps back from the camera and claps his hands. Missy and I blush, lost in our world, forgetting our observer.

"Let me see," I say and Missy walks with me eagerly.

"Look," says Trey, scrolling through the pictures, all of them which are perfect. The sun paints our hair and the teardrop leaves. It's a vanilla lilac sky behind us and Trey captures the moment, our candid smiles, and the longing in our eyes. The last photo is of our kiss. It's sweet as well as romantic but has an air of secrecy.

"Thank you," I say in a rasp. For some reason I want to cry.

—Tawnya Torres—

Cabin Pressure

—Kevin Foote

Ooone, Twooo Threee, Four!
The noggin-head behind my seat proudly counts out her harbinger melody
With each number squealed as the plane ramps up
she tells me:
This is not just a poem of grief.
It is a poem of hope, okay? Kay!

Look! Her voice trails over
growling engine and gathering storm
Her singular whimper as her ears pop
beckons, gathers me
Beside and above rain pouring over Littleton
Lightning kisses earth
heading towards Bear Valley
and she tells me:

To be a teacher
is to lay down your weapons, forever
To be a little girl
dreams like gossamer cinched like seatbelts
through the herky-jerky ride
singing your numbers through it.

To be a farmer
in mists of morning
To be a farmer
in mists of mourning

She giggles over yet another empty
milk carton that *pop, pop-pops*
under foot that you think is gunfire for the tenth time this week so your eyes are weeping in pre-harvest fog so thick they
slick clothes and masks windshields and desk shields
dried soil and dying stars
twenty to forty of them
Looking back at you.

—Kevin Foote—

To be a rock
in the river as it floods
unwavering
yet flows the right way
because of you
knees and shoulders bent over at attention
singular and immovable
smoothing until your corners disappear

She cough-coughs on her snack cart Coke
and tells me once more before watching Peppa Pig

To be a teacher
is to be a storm chaser
not the quiet nor the calm
but there–with her–and there wherever she will go
until the storm takes
one of you.

—Kevin Foote—

Falling

—Andi Benet

—Andi Benet—

Unbelonging
  —S. Kavi

keep your mouth shut you are a shame we don't claim her you are not truly Indian no wonder the stereotype exists angry brown girl എന്തൊരു നാണക്കടേ keep your mouth shut you are a shame we don't claim her white-washed you are not truly Indian no wonder the stereotype exists angry brown girl എന്തൊരു നാണക്കടേ keep your mouth shut you are a shame we don't claim her white-washed you are not truly Indian no wonder the stereotype exists angry brown girl എന്തൊരു നാണക്കടേ keep your mouth shut you are a shame we don't claim her white-washed you are not truly Indian no wonder the stereotype exists angry brown girl എന്തൊരു നാണക്കടേ keep your mouth shut you are a shame we don't claim her white-washed you are not truly Indian no wonder the stereotype exists angry brown girl എന്തൊരു നാണക്കടേ keep your mouth shut you are a shame we don't claim her you are not truly Indian no wonder the stereotype exists angry brown girl എന്തൊരു നാണക്കടേ keep your mouth shut you are a shame we don't claim her white-washed you are not truly Indian no wonder the stereotype exists angry brown girl എന്തൊരു നാണക്കടേ keep your mouth shut you are a shame we don't claim her white-washed you are not truly Indian no wonder the stereotype exists angry brown girl എന്തൊരു നാണക്കടേ keep your mouth shut you are a shame we don't claim her white-washed you are not truly Indian no wonder the stereotype exists angry brown girl എന്തൊരു നാണക്കടേ keep your mouth shut you are a shame we don't claim her you are not truly Indian no wonder the stereotype exists angry brown girl എന്തൊരു നാണക്കടേ keep your mouth shut you are a shame we don't claim her white-washed you are not truly Indian no wonder the stereotype exists angry brown girl എന്തൊരു നാണക്കടേ keep your mouth shut you are a shame we don't claim her white-washed you are not truly Indian no wonder the stereotype exists angry brown girl എന്തൊരു നാണക്കടേ keep your mouth shut you are a shame we don't claim her white-washed you are not truly Indian no wonder the stereotype exists angry brown girl എന്തൊരു നാണക്കടേ keep your mouth shut you are a shame we don't claim her you are not truly Indian no wonder the stereotype exists angry brown girl എന്തൊരു നാണക്കടേ keep your mouth shut you are a shame we don't claim her white-washed you are not truly Indian no wonder the stereotype exists angry brown girl എന്തൊരു നാണക്കടേ keep your mouth shut you are a shame we don't claim her you are not truly Indian

Divorcing

—Robert Allen

Prior to our divorce proceedings, we took a few weeks away from each other before the final split, when we would move to different states. During those weeks I escaped to southern France, and she took a long road trip in her old van. We were both running but my plane would come home, her trip would end, and we'd have to see each other again.

The meeting to divide our things was rough as sandpaper, as neither of us wanted to be there, but we had to get this done so we could each move on. The state we lived in, Washington, required us to swear that our marriage was "irretrievably broken." We had been broken for a long time but the words were hard to say, like some sort of dark poetry, an admission of defeat.

Who gets what then? A small tiff around Eliot's Collected Poems and some other books we loved together, a painting of a cross on the wall, some music. No agreement about the dishes, the furniture, our bed. No kids, no cats. Dividing was still harder on us both than we had imagined. What do you do with the food, late bills, leftover desire?

Division brings thirst, for the past, or for booze, for the desire for something to go down hard. I opened the fridge for a drink and saw a clear Tupperware container with a blue green nest inside, which had once been food. Furred algae. The promise of stink. We joked that it was a metaphor for us. Which brought a smile to the dark day.

She left. I was alone in the house and it ached. My heart was full of echoes. I was other-minded and forgot about the poison in the refrigerator. Two days later I took it out to toss it away outside but the lid came loose, and it unfurled like a flag.

The stench hung around for weeks.

Dreaming

   —Robin Williams

Summer Fruit
  —*Robin Williams*

Ex

—*Ellen Clayton*

Ex

We have stood, hip to hip, giggling
at the sink — I watched you spit
toothpaste and blood, freaked out
when I saw the mouthwash advert
with a dire warning of tooth loss
and begged you to visit the dentist.

You were by my side (needing
to stay close on that dark, frozen night)
as I squatted in the snow,
both of us looking down in grim fascination
as steam rose and snow melted.

How is it possible that we shared
that level of intimacy
and I don't even know where
you live now? Are your gums and teeth ok?
~~Do you ever think of me?~~

—*Ellen Clayton*—

11 Ways to Hurt Yourself

—Anna Louise Steig

1. Fling your body from the Brooklyn Bridge and watch as passing Subarus speed by unaware.
2. Forget about the overdue essay and burn a mixtape for your plug instead; he gives you discounts just because you're pretty and you're loose.
3. Run the bathwater to a boil and pretend you're soup. Scrub until the skin comes off to reveal the bone and become pure.
4. Donate your trust fund to the Trevor Project.
5. Kiss your best friend, but only after the sun has gone down and she won't be able to see your sober smile.
6. Join the circus.
7. Go to college.
8. Stub out a cigarette on your wrist just to see if it burns. If it does, do it again.
9. Tell your father you forgive him.
10. Get a job and stop writing poetry on the sides of coffee cups.
11. Eat dirt and cry about it.

the longest apologies

—J.I. Kleinberg

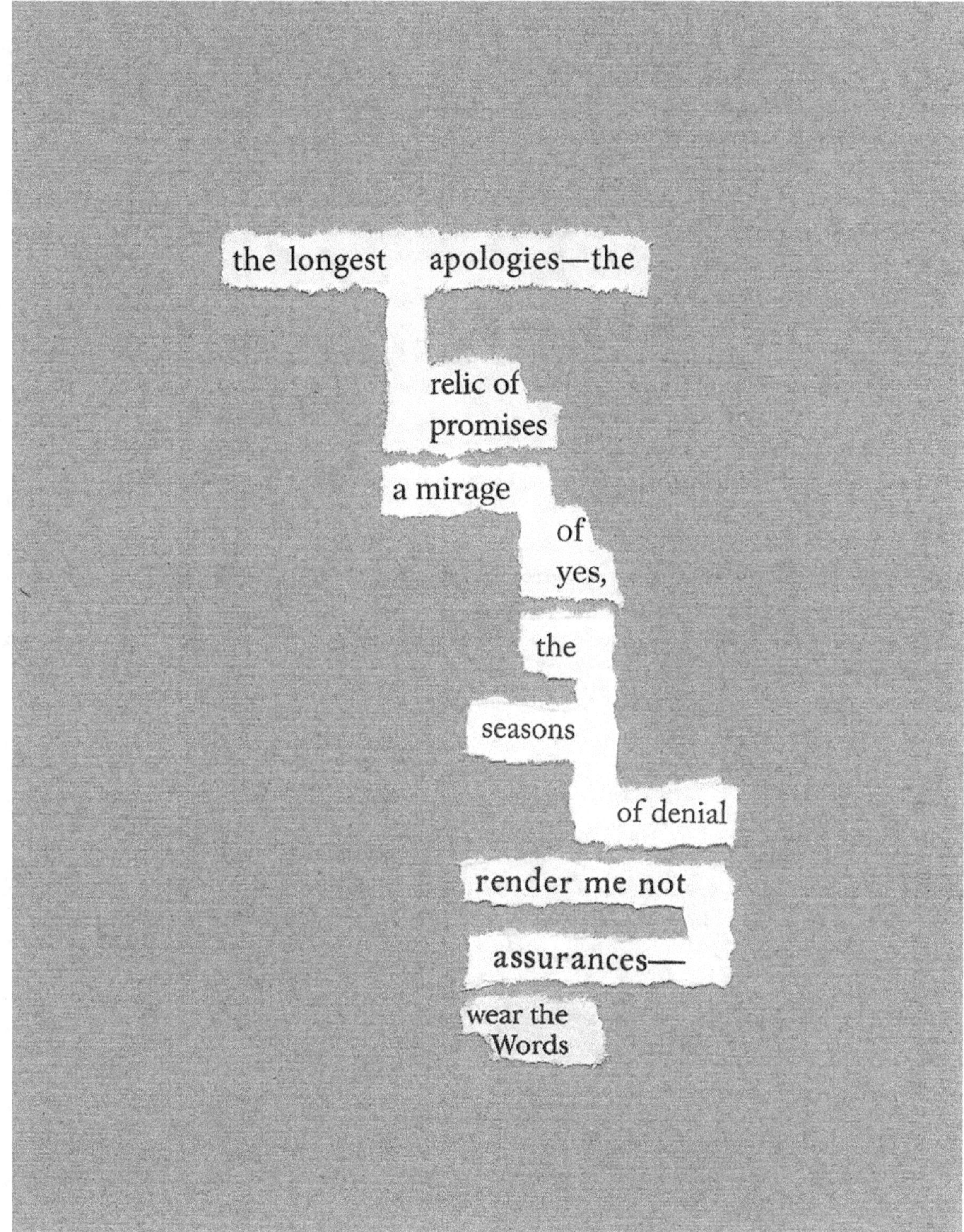

—J.I. Kleinberg—

The Redo

—Julie Stenton

"I have something for you," the man says, his heavy glasses slipping down an outlandishly long nose. *"It's a chance of sorts, a second one, so to speak."* My interest is piqued, in fact the guy would have my full attention if I could just stop thinking about reaching out to push his frames up a little higher. *"Are you listening?"* he asks, and goes on to say in a somewhat stern voice that this second chance is a one-off – it won't come around again – and that I am to choose just one moment of a day in my entire life, a single thing to change – to be redone – if I so wish.

I don't have much time to think – there was a last-minute cancellation you see, and the redo must happen tomorrow. He sees himself out with these parting words, and I'm paraphrasing here but the gist of it is, *"Go with your gut, there must be something that sticks out."* I write your name on the palm of my left hand in red ink and go to sleep with a clenched fist.

And when I wake up, it's exactly as I remember. The sky is grey and the streets are wet – I won't be changing this because, although I hate the rain, you quite fancy it. We had agreed to meet at Stardust Diner at ten, not my first choice but it was convenient, I seem to recall. And you're more than an hour late because of a flat tire – I don't change that part either because the coffee at Stardust is actually okay and I don't mind waiting for you. I actually love waiting for you. And then you arrive. Your hug is warm. Your hair's a mess – my word it's worse than I remember. Your pants are cute – cream with blue stripes – your ass looks fantastic in those damn pants, I wouldn't change them for love nor money. We both eat eggs and avocado and then we leave.

You say you want to take a trip so we get into my car, on account of yours being on the side of a road somewhere, and we drive for three hours and twelve minutes and listen to four full albums. At this point your throat is sore and your voice is raspy in that way that I like, and you're laughing and gently touching my hand, and there's no way I'm changing any of that because it was all fucking perfect if you ask me. But then we pull off at a look-out so that we can – look out – at the glorious scene beneath us. And just as you peer over the edge a gust of wind sweeps past taking your hat with it, into the abyss below.

And my god – the look on your face – you're distraught and you keep saying over and over how much you love that hat, and that your mother gave it to you, and you're looking at me with ocean-blue eyes, wet and salty, and I say, *"It's okay – it's just a hat."* And it's immediately clear that it is absolutely not just a hat and how could I possibly have said that? And all I can hear is the man with the nose and those glasses telling me to trust my instincts, or something along those lines, and so this – this is what I change – I make it so that you left the hat at home. But as soon as I change it I realise I've made a terrible mistake. Because now your scarf has blown away, and you don't even really care. And we're still driving home in silence. And you still never touch my hand again.

I Want to Talk

 —Julie Stenton

I want to talk to you, like, really talk, but when you get home I can't remember what I wanted to say and instead I tell you that I've put fresh towels in the bathroom. You know how some mornings you walk under a streetlamp at the precise moment that it turns off? When that happens it makes me feel like anything is possible. Every blade of grass is encased in a fine layer of frost. It crunches underfoot and I can't shake the thought that I am breaking something. How many meaningful sentences have you uttered today? Does it even matter? Was the conversation always going to happen like this? No, I did not empty the lint filter in the tumble dryer and I'm honestly very sorry. The streetlamp turns off and the ground beneath it is no longer illuminated. A new day floats into the air, coating the trees with light that spins in all directions.

Summer in Michigan

—Michele Gorman

solitaire sang
   —Emily Ruth Verona

a lacerated heart
steeped in lavender.

nutmeg nociceptors,
roasted lightly.

brutalities broiled.
potential preened.

earthy, luscious—sharp.
a pulmonary profile.

parfum de
solitaire sang.

—Emily Ruth Verona—

Fractured Nursery Rhymes

—Betty-Jo Tilley

I started seeing Evelyn Mirman, Ph.D., Psychology, at the suggestion of a girlfriend. "She doesn't just listen," she said, "she really tells you what to do." This is what I needed, I thought, a pro trainer to teach me how to toughen up. How to be a big girl in the business world, because Tom Wick was never going to stop yelling. I would leave Memory Lane out of it. No sense having her wonder if I was all there.

I liked her the second I saw her. She had a hard face, a chiseled, pointed jaw line, and direct eyes. She looked smart. And tough. Like she could deliver a low blow and not get all girly about it. She sat in her chair with her legs curled under her butt. Like she didn't give a shit if you thought she was a lady or not.

She got straight to business the moment I sat down. "So tell me," she posed her question as a demand, not fooling around, "Why are you here." She was direct and I liked that. I could be direct, too, if I was paying her a dollar and a half a minute, which I was.

"I can't stop crying at work," I told her. "My boss is a yeller. He's got a cigarette hanging out of his mouth every second of the day. He's scarier than shit."

She studied me. I hoped she wouldn't ask why he frightened me so. "Okay, so tell me exactly, what is it that you want."

"I want to be a barracuda businesswoman." I could tell that appealed to her when her shin bobbed slightly up and down. This egged me on. "I think I've got it in me."

Three months of weekly sessions with Evelyn and I felt I could just about have Tom Wick begging me for a job. She made me feel my bravado was mine, not just a figment of my imagination. I told her I'd made up some fractured nursery rhymes to keep from taking him seriously. She clapped her hands while bouncing up and down in her easy chair, cheering me on. "You've got it in you, alright," she said. "That's brilliant! You've got to emasculate him in your mind! That is your homework," she said. She gestured toward the door with a satisfied grin, "Good work, we're done for the day. Next week, I want you to bring in your nursery rhyme and you're going to chant it like a mantra whenever you feel like crying. It will be like Transcendental Meditation!" She giggled, and I giggled too. Contrary to the tension I'd felt about my job, it was becoming fun for me. I couldn't wait to share my rhymes with Evelyn, and it delighted me to think of her reaction.

She settled into her big chair as soon as I sat down. I stared at her foot as I launched right into my recital. I wanted to see her bounce up and down and giggle.

Thomas Wickit what a pricket,
Had a dick but couldn't stick it.
If he knew her very well, his little dick just wouldn't swell.
If he loved her more than all, his dick would hide between his balls.
Poor Thomas Wickit what a prickit. Had a dick but couldn't stick it.

—Betty-Jo Tilley—

"Yes!" she shouted and pumped her arms up and down, "Atta Girl!" as if I, her favorite middle weight, had just delivered a one and done.

"I've got more," I added. Her foot jiggled happily. I was on a roll now.

Little Tommy Wickit, sat in a thickit,

Eating a ciggy pie.

He put in his tongue,

It tasted like scum,

And said, "What a big prick am I."

"Go with both of 'em!" and she clapped her hands in succession while bouncing in her seat with a super gleeful look on her face.

I laughed and clapped my hands, too. This was going to work, I knew it.

—Betty-Jo Tilley—

Don't Grow Up Darling
—*Rose Kendall*

—*Rose Kendall*—

The Day My Mom Died
   —*Chad Diamond Dann*

There was a big red truck in the driveway. I walked up brown wooden stairs. My dad, hunched over in my mom's blue chair, lifted his head, tears in his eyes. Green planters swung from the metallic tin-roof porch. Cigarette butts overflowed like a clogged toilet in the ashtray.

A black sky with traces of moonlight filled the trailer park. If there were stars, I didn't see them. Blinded by tears, I looked through hazy clouds.

The white screen door with the silver handle was the way inside. A tungsten bulb shined bright above, lighting the way to the darkest place I would ever travel.

—Chad Diamond Dann—

religious scrupulosity
   —Willow Page Delp

religious scrupulosity is when you cry over a god that you no longer

believe in. (to be fair, you cry over yourself, and you have abandoned that

wasteland centuries ago, its remnants slowly possessed by

rot.) you take your chances elsewhere, in the heavenly arms of a deity, yet His imagined

presence provides you with nothing but his ever-present eyes and his

disappointment. you worship

when you bleed and you bleed

when you worship. *none of this is real.* but there's always Pascal

and his pesky wager, lurking within the pages of every

bible, every worn book of prayers.

Fish Pond

—Rose Kendall

—Rose Kendall—

Advice to the New Mother Sitting Next to Me in the Airport Lounge
—Elaine Westnott-O'Brien

Rule number one:
    ignore all advice.

Nobody knows your particular rips and scars, your new healing birth wounds, how they stretch and pull as you stand to rock your infant by the coffee machine. Nobody understands the tiny person that you have carried, and carry, and will carry, better than you do. More importantly, nobody else will carry that child, in all their iterations, in the same way you will. Your particular carrying can only be done by you, in your particular way, and that is enough.

Rule number two:
    ignore all opinions.

Everybody has a voice, and God bless them, they are free to use it. You are free to nod and smile, or look away, free to focus on the snowdrop breaths of your nascent bud, nestled close to your chest. It is their voiceless opinion that matters, nonverbal but strident in its expression.

Rule number three:
    ignore your hunger, your thirst, your exhaustion, at your peril.

Listen to your growling, savage desire, do not tame it. It will always come second now, but it cannot be silenced. Feed it with what it needs to grow; don't throw it scraps. It is changing, becoming other, becoming mother. It needs sustenance, just as much as that little creature you bounce and rock.

Rule number four:
    priority boarding should now be yours forever.

It won't, because we don't cherish mothers, we fail to see how much they stand and sway and listen for cries, even when their babies are not near, or are grown, or are gone. I see you tensely scooping vegetable soup into your untasting mouth, watching as your partner walks the baby around so you can get a moment. No moment is ever yours though, not fully. Even when you are in an airport lounge, sipping lattes at your leisure, and your children are not with you, you will listen for them, wonder if they have eaten raisins or bananas, drunk too much, slept too little. You will watch other children with other mothers, feeling your heart contract and bloom, a thousand miles away.

—Elaine Westnott-O'Brien—

Rule number five:

      each moment is a flower of impermanence, budding, blooming, gently rotting away.

Know that there is regrowth in spring. It won't be the same flower, but it will be enriched by colours and textures of all the flowers that softly crumpled here before. Wrap your baby close, wrap yourself close, and board that flight, safe in the knowledge that you will be held, suspended in the air, that gravity will not have its way with you. There will be turbulence, and you will always

                bump,

                    bump,

                        bump

back to earth, but in the in-between,
you will soar.

—Elaine Westnott-O'Brien—

Suicide Erasure: Virginia Woolf

—LindaAnn LoSchiavo

Erasure: Dearest Vanessa

Virginia Woolf's suicide note to her sister Vanessa Bell, written on March 23, 1941.

Sunday

Dearest, You can't think how ① loved your letter. But I feel I have gone too far this time to **come back** again. I am certain now that I am going mad again. It is just as it was the **first** time, I am always hearing voices, and I shan't get over it now. All I want **to** say is that Leonard has been so astonishingly **good**, every day, always ① can't **imagine** that anyone could have done **more** for me than he has. We have been **perfectly** happy until these last few weeks, when this horror began. Will you assure him of this? I feel he has so much to do that he will go on, better without me **and** you will help him. I can hardly think **clearly** anymore. If I could I would tell you what you and the children have meant to me. I think you know. I have fought against it, but I can't any longer. — Virginia

— —

On March 28, 1941, shortly after the start of WWII, British writer Virginia Woolf (January 25, 1882 – March 28, 1941) filled her overcoat pockets with rocks and walked into the River Ouse behind her country home – Monk's House, Rodmell, Lewes, East Sussex, England – never to emerge alive.

During their long marriage, her husband Leonard had nursed her through multiple suicide attempts and mental breakdowns. But an all-consuming depression had resurfaced. She was 59 years old.

Virginia left behind three suicide notes, two for her husband Leonard Woolf and one for her sister, Vanessa Bell. One suicide note is quoted here.

Suicide Erasure: Ida Craddock

—LindaAnn LoSchiavo

Ida Craddock's Letter to her Mother on the Day of her Suicide
New York, Oct. 16, 1902

Dear, Dear Mother:

I know you will grieve over me for having taken my life.... My dear, dear mother, oh, how sorry I am to hurt you, as I know this act will do. But, oh, mother, I cannot, I will not consent to go to the asylum, as you are evidently planning to have me go. I know that this means a perpetual imprisonment all my long life, unless I either recant my religious beliefs or else hypocritically pretend to do so. I cannot bring myself to consent to any of these three alternatives. I maintain my right to die as I have lived, a free woman, not cowed into silence by any other human being. If, on the other hand, the prison to which Judge Thomas evidently proposes to send me were to be the death penalty (and I know very well that he wishes and means to lock me up for as long a time as he legally can, if not actually my death warrant), my work is ended here so far as this world is concerned, I have been given a start, approved by physicians and, the world is not yet ready for all the beautiful teachings. Some one will take up my work, however, some day, and will start from where I left off and do better work than I. Some day you'll be proud of me. You will understand it all because you and my father prepared me for just such a fate. You may ask why I did not give it up and come home to live the name of "Miss Craddock," and taking up other work, would be of no possible help to you, with the shadow of reproach which narrow-minded people have put on me. I should be only a hindrance to you. Moreover, my individuality has some rights. I cannot recant my beliefs and the principle for which I have toiled and struggled for nine years, even at the behest of a mother that is dear to me.

Do not grieve, dear, dear mother; the world beyond the grave, believe me, is far more real and substantial than is this world in which we to-day live. This earth life which the Hindoos have for centuries termed *Maya*, but it is illusion. My people assure me ...

— —

Raised in Philadelphia, Ida C. Craddock [August 1, 1857 – October 16, 1902] was a 19th-century advocate of free speech and women's rights and an erotic mystic. From her office at 134 West 23rd St., Room 5, New York, NY, Craddock wrote extensively on sexuality, inspired by her noisy sexual sessions with Soph, her ghost lover. To avoid going to prison for mailing "obscene" books she had written, she explained her situation in two suicide letters, then slit her wrists and inhaled gas from a stove. She was 45 years old.

Prayer

—Andi Benet

—Andi Benet—

Freaks, or Too Many Kitties and Cherries
   —Lauren Emily Whalen

We are a sparkly bunch of freaks. We are perpetually broke and always hustling, with two or three or five or seven different jobs at once. We live in Chicago, most of us, and spend most of our time on public transit or in our cars, always on the move to the next gig or job or date or appointment.

We're late, we're late, we're constantly freaking *late*. We dress as white rabbits and showgirls and Han Solo on the weekends, slowly shedding our costume pieces to carefully chosen music until we're in nothing but glitter and lace, stilettos or combat boots or bare feet. We roll around in glitter on barroom floors, beat our faces to the goddesses in tiny restroom stalls or back rooms that are little more than a hole in the floor with a candle beside it. We always carry hand mirrors, carry extra wig tape for our pasties and those around us, carry the 1 when we're adding up tip money.

We help each other get jobs, waiting tables at brunch spots, temping in downtown offices of chrome and glass, helping nervous brides find the perfect discount gown. We reach out to one another through Facebook text Instagram DM to console after a gig gone wrong or a pastie pop, to congratulate on "slaying" an audition that we didn't end up booking, to pass along an email of a producer who needs a last minute replacement for a Saturday night show that's in the burbs, but it pays! We talk stage names, bad sex, good sex, vegan cooking, our next solo act we're submitting to the next solo festival, as we slap sequined covers on our nipples, sequined patches on our privates, sequined shoes on our tired feet. We cry between our first act and our second because the hustle is just so goddamn exhausting and our partners are getting tired of us not being home till very late, and when our music starts, we slap on a smile that's real.

We pose for artists, in our costumes or nude or a bespoke combo of both, because god knows modeling pays better than performing, really *anything* pays better than performing. But we love it so so so much, are addicted to the spotlight even if it comes from someone's phone in a barroom basement or the filter is so shitty our skin looks disastrously pasty. We are not your average shes and gays and theys. We don't know what average is, but we're pretty sure we'd hate it.

We know who we are, and in burlesque, that starts with your name. Not your birth/government/muggle name. Your stage name: the one you choose. And you better choose carefully: your name is your brand, your identity, your destiny. Google the shit out of it and all iterations to make sure there's not an award-winning dancer in Amsterdam using the same name. Also? Avoid felines and red fruit.

"Too many Kitties and Cherries!" I told my writing workshop, referring to the ubiquity of these two monikers. They don't know this world, and I'm doing my best to outline all the particularities I and my community take for granted. "The new dancers think they're being clever, or sexy, and I *was* new once, but my god, if I never see another Kitty or Cherry…"

My burlesque name was, *is*, Emma Glitterbomb. Not the cleverest or punniest or most glamorous, but me through and through.

Emma: a reference to a line from the play *Sex With Strangers* where the main character is struggling for a nom de plume, and bandies around the name Emily, and her writer-lover who's based on Tucker Max says, "Emma's sexier than Emily." I had a writer-lover around the time I saw the play. My middle name is Emily. Done.

Glitterbomb: a reference to the TV show *Parks and Recreation*, which I stopped watching after season three because it got too cutesy. Wannabe fuckboy Tom Haverford is depressed and wants to go to a strip club, and the cheesy DJ yells "GLITTERBOMB!" right when Ron Swanson is enjoying the complimentary breakfast buffet, and thus is forced to cover his pancakes. I didn't have a pancake-lover at the time. I just liked the word.

—Lauren Emily Whalen—

Before I started performing, I went to the New Year's Eve show of the troupe I would eventually join, with a friend from burlesque class. Someone asked us our stage names. "Emma Glitterbomb" danced out of my mouth, and I knew that was me.

We know who we are. We brave freezing rain and falling snow and blistering heat to get mostly naked for you. We grin through cramps and limp through sprains and before the pandemic we performed with colds that we tried not to give our siblings in sparkle. We know to tuck our tampon strings or just cut them off, because yes, we do have to perform on our periods and we can't believe you'd ask that, who are we, Marilyn Monroe? When one of us *does* have to cancel, to call in, another is at the ready, armed with extra pastie tape and safety thongs and a shiny brand-new act, ready to slap on falsies (eyelashes, not boobs, though sometimes boobs) and pocket that unexpected coin.

We are used to being used, by partners by producers by predatory photographers. Doesn't mean we like it. Our whisper network is strong but could be stronger, because loyalty is a funny thing and moles are real. Even anonymous reports sometimes get back to the last possible person. We protect each other as best we can though. We try. We know how vulnerable this art form makes even the strongest-willed and thick-skinned of us all, and how the wrong comment can have us questioning every single decision, especially the biggest one of all—to put it all out there in nothing but a G-string.

Most of all we are passionate we are stunning we are free we are named.

We know who we are.

—Lauren Emily Whalen—

The Ephemeral
—*Kushal Poddar*

The paying guest college kid

sinks his teeth in his

morning pizza, the first order

of the day for Mrs. Ray's.

The porch shines beneath

the newsworthy clear sky.

The paper reports about a city

choking on orange air.

Not this one we have today.

We too have the other kind of blue

when lungs shrink and hearts hurt.

I watch the kid. A flying ant writhes

on the cheese melt. The red

of the tomatoes stream to no place.

—Kushal Poddar—

Winged
  —*Rachel Coyne*

—*Rachel Coyne*—

Eat It!

—Lori D'Angelo

Though Jimmy was egging her on, and Kaylee liked Jimmy, Kaylee did not want to eat it.

"It's *just* a bug," he said.

"Yeah," she said. She knew it was just a bug. But she had heard that eating dead bugs led to ingesting all sorts of raw and unsavory things from roadkill birds to severed squirrels to Creatures from the Deep.

Creatures from the Deep, of course, were anything that lived in Coven Lake. Coven Lake was a special, terrible place. So many people had gone there on innocent, paradise type holidays, back when Ravensboro was a tourist town rather than a place for paranormal haunts, and never returned.

Truthfully, Kaylee liked it better this way. The types of tourists they got before were so irritatingly suburban with their yoga pants and selfie sticks and their single-serve low-fat high-protein smoothies that Kaylee couldn't abide them because they were so far removed from the nose to the grind real world that Kaylee knew.

Kaylee had dropped out of high school last year at 15 to work at the Ravensboro Inn, which was owned by her grandparents. Her mother, lost to addiction before Kaylee could remember, didn't work, didn't do much of anything. When Kaylee was five, her grandparents took her in and kept her, and she was grateful for that, but they expected her to earn her keep.

So she worked at the inn, checking in guests, cleaning rooms, stripping beds, and stocking the breakfast bar. The breakfast room, where the inn served its free subpar continental breakfast, which consisted mainly of packet hot chocolate, Nutri-Grain bars, low quality danishes, and sugar cereal, was where she and Jimmy sat now, around one of the round wood tables where guests gathered to eat and stuff their purses with bite sized bulk ordered mini muffins and packets of Celestial Seasonings Tea.

Kaylee flicked the fly between her fingers like a paperclip still trying to determine if she would stick it in her mouth. "If I eat it for you," Kaylee asked suggestively, "what will you do for me?"

Sometimes, when Kaylee looked at Jimmy, she didn't know why she liked him. Maybe it was because he didn't remind her of any of the losers Kaylee saw her mother with, when she saw her mother at all. Her grandparents didn't like her to see her mother because they didn't think she was a good influence. Kaylee questioned their parenting skills though because they were the ones who had raised her mother, and look how she had turned out. Unlike the heavily tattooed gaunt looking men that Kaylee's mother hung out with, Jimmy was fleshy, substantial, uninked. He didn't look like he would fade away with the next gusty wind from over the lake. She wanted to know what it was like to hold a body like that, big and bulky.

"What do you want?" Jimmy asked while he watched Kaylee play with the fly.

Kaylee hesitated for a second, then she said it. The worst he could say was no.

"I want you to let me suck your dick," Kaylee said.

Jimmy shrugged, as if it was no big deal, as if girls asked him to let them to do that every single day. "Okay," Jimmy said.

Kaylee shoved the fly into her mouth and bit into it. It was crunchy, like fried chicken, and didn't even taste half bad.

After she was done chewing, Jimmy asked where, and she directed him to Room 12, which was where Kaylee went to do all the things she shouldn't do when she wanted to do them: masturbate, watch sex movies, drink. What could she say? Her grandparents didn't know how to raise a teenager, and they never even found her once. She didn't think they had even tried. Plus, in case her grandparents suddenly became all helicoptery or interested, Kaylee always locked the deadbolt.

Kaylee knew what to do from the sex movies she had seen. But seeing was different than doing, and she was surprised how easy it was to get his penis hard. The only questions Kaylee had thought she'd have now was whether, when Jimmy's penis began flowing like a river, she would swallow or spit. What she hadn't anticipated when she had imagined this was the sound of Jimmy's soft moaning and how badly she wanted to bite down on him like she had done with the bug.

—Lori D'Angelo—

pain relief
—Skylar Miklus

not only joints not only knees not only hips but a glistening highway of pain roars sternum to insoled insides of my shoes I bear it all I bear eighteen-wheelers grinding over each vertebra with care I bear asphalt shrink-wrapped around my breasts I google symptoms of a heart attack I have to scroll to page two before I google symptoms of a heart attack *female* I google duloxetine pain relief I google pregabalin pain gabapentin pain amitriptyline citalopram lamotrigine bupropion milnacipran fluoxetine cyclobenzaprine pain I ask what is the difference between relief and prevention I ask what is the difference between mental and physical health I ask what if improving one makes the other disintegrate I study the diagram of the nervous system I trace the vagus nerve from gut to brain and back again I trace the flow of chemicals that respond to each of my triggers like gas stations bus stations elevators highways garages basements like men at night like men in general I shudder I wonder if this is why it's called gut feeling

Home is Nature

—*Roya Motazedian*

—Roya Motazedian—

Grief is a broken wine glass

—Fortune Simeon Eleojo

thrown at you/at every bisection/of your
      shadow
              My lover says/my
breath/is a   hot   eraser
     on   a   cobweb/
  of broken
            hearts
At the cathedral/
     on   the   eve/
of your/
       boyfriend's birthday
  you   arched/   your
     hopes
into   /dissected
    alphabets
that sings into/
        grief
 This poem   is/
      not   about
love
   it's about/the   soprano   of/
       your heart's
melodies
    that   breaks
a wine glass
  But your/   prom dress/
   is a rag/in your   boyfriend's house

"images"
   —Melissa Palumbo

i said i like the color pink, like blushing roses and being flushed from snow, i like femme styling and strawberry drinks.

yesterday my shirt was blue; i could feel a change in your attitude, between me and my shifting identity.

please stop observing me.

we forcefully forge our paths in this world yet each morning we dress ourselves in labels, and the images we paint of ourselves are subject to change without warning.

avoid your truth for a night, avoid your reflection for life — how do you identify?

will it be the same in a year, a decade? is it even the same as yesterday? please don't make me define it, but if i had to describe it…

i suppose i see myself as a beautiful, flowering plant, maybe an abelia or a morning glory vine, that has been burned more than a few times. scorched, smoldered, i was incinerated down to the ground but my roots are strong.

that's how i identify.

Whispers of the Reef
—*Jenna Johnson*

Acrylic on Canvas
16"x20"

—Judge Kemp Jr.

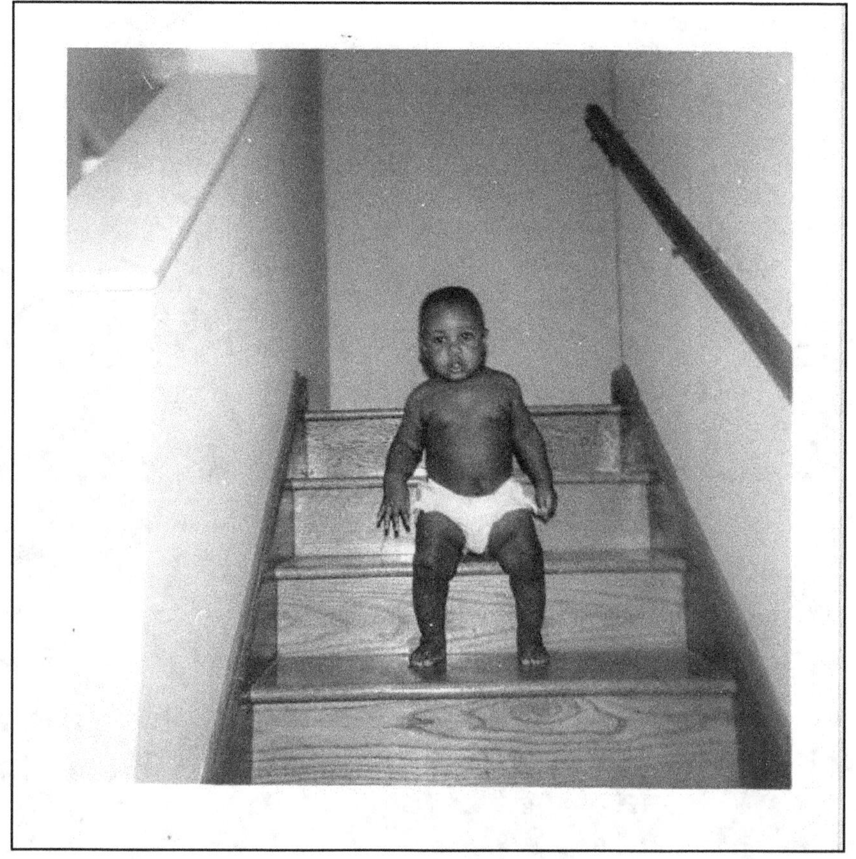

XY

12:26 AM Monday
17th day of month 8 in year 64
expelled from place warm
a sanctuary, a chamber of love, of life
into a space, a world cold, uncertainty, a time of joy
sensations new of air, in light, and smell
a detachment of umbilical nourishment, snip
confirmed se**X**
fingerling digits and appendages checked, snip and smack
cries of pain and fear subside
as voice, female, and familiar calls out in exhaustion
give him to me, she says
you are my bo**Y**

Black Birds of Sorrow

—Irina Tall (Novikova)

—Irina Tall (Novikova)—

The World Came From an Egg

—Irina Tall (Novikova)

—Irina Tall (Novikova)—

Flamingo

—Gemma Elliott

It started when the arches of my feet were getting too old for standing at gigs. I was still wearing fashionable flat soled shoes then, and I noticed that I couldn't last through the whole concert without shifting from foot to foot to foot to foot. Over and over, relieving the ache with every swap. It got me through the encores and home by public transport. But in time I had painful strains the next morning too, and then they were lasting for days, creeping up my calves and thighs until I hurt all over.

'Yoga's the answer,' a colleague convinced me, effusive after finishing a month of daily sessions. The yoga did help, following videos online of a friendly woman with a soothing voice. I flexed my feet and my legs. I kicked through from downward facing dog into a lunge then warrior two. I got into a habit of doing it before bed to relax.

An unexpected benefit of my new exercise regime was that my balance improved along with my strengthened legs. So, when my feet did start to ache a little towards the end of nights out, I could confidently give each side a rest by tucking my tired foot into eagle pose behind the standing leg.

Garudasana, I learned my favourite pose was officially called with more research into my newest obsession. Most yogis called it the eagle, but I felt more like a flamingo. They say that flamingos keep half their brain awake while they sleep on one leg. I wondered if I could do that too.

I visited the flamingos at the local zoo on a day off and found them quite calming to observe, occasionally tucking in one leg then the other as I grew weary. On my sixth visit in a month, having taken days off work for fictional dental treatments and family emergencies, I heard a child whisper 'mummy that lady is copying the pink birds,' and that was the end of that.

In private was a different matter though. I had bought a standing desk so that I could be on one leg, giving each side a fair turn, throughout the working day. Sitting just wasn't doing it for me anymore, it felt like a waste. I couldn't quite convince my brain to copy the flamingos' lead and give me a side at a time in sleep, but muscle memory is strong and eventually I could go to sleep one-legged and wake up still standing. It took a few falls but I got there. Each night I lock one knee in to position, shut off my whole brain, and I rest.

—Gemma Elliott—

Spiral
—Roya Motazedian

every time i wake up the sky is grey outside again but i still have hope. i still have hope until the hours have drained me and i wish i hadn't woken up at all. i wonder why i even bother trying. i wonder why i'm even here when i haven't left the house in a week and no one likes talking to me anymore. the last time i heard my voice was when you spoke. i don't know how it feels to go home anymore; i've been living in this rotting house of a soul for two decades now. i wish someone would just take me home but everyone's so busy. i hate the word 'busy'. it's so inhumane and dull to be busy. i want to be busy too, but with you. yet, it seems everyone else prefers being busy without me. i'm no longer an excuse for you to get out of plans. i'm the one you send excuses to to get out of meeting me. and i guess that's sign number one of a fractured friendship, of a home that's beginning to look like it'll slam its door in your face. i am a sleepwalker, a zombie, i keep walking, keep chasing even though no one wants me there. this is just who i am. would you accept me like this? i accepted your bruised soul from the start so won't you think of me at all? no, you view me as a book, not a soul. you've opened me up, read all there is to see and now you rip me up, page by page. you slam my own cover shut, burn me, chuck me at your wall. since homes are built so violently, with trees cut down and pollution sent up, do i have to endure a beat-down just to find a home as well? it's not just me, right? you're lying when you say you're visiting your grandpa, right? you're just like me, right? you also have no family on this side of the world, right? you're also dying of loneliness, right? you also scare your friends away with the poems disguised as texts that you send them, right? i know it's not just me. i know you're putting on an act. good! because it's one thing to be lonely… being lonely together is so much nicer than being lonely alone. let's sit beside each other and cry at the moon that never dares show its face because of all the wishes it never granted us. let's let's let's but really i'm just talking to the mirror because i'm lonely, alone. always on my own. the only home i'll ever know.

—Roya Motazedian—

Zone Out
—Auguste Fallon

—Auguste Fallon—

Start the New Year by Watching The Hustler
  —*Ace Boggess*

The right movie for looking back at 2020:
it hits the angles, trick shots;
it begins with glory that leads to grief,
ends on the same two beats, &
a kind of love that's broken, terrible.
I'm at home in this film with its rapid swings &
depravity minus judgment.
In the cringeworthy scene as thugs shatter
Fast Eddie's thumbs, I consider the middle
of last year & its violent hopelessness,
virus squeezing us against a window.
Later: death, grief, lashing out. Yet,
there was tenderness among the damaged,
then, despite perceived triumph,
a promise of more suffering to come.

THE WORD OF GOD
— Daniel Schulz

GOOD MORNING,

I AM NOT IN GOOD SHAPE. A LOT OF PAIN 24/7 THEY CANNOT INCREASE THE OPIOIDS BECAUSE MY BLADDER WILL NOT WORK. THIS IS WHAT HAPPENS WHEN PEOPLE FEED YOU TOO MUCH PROPAGANDA. I WANT/NEED OPIUM. I HAVE MACULA DEGENERATION IN BOTH EYES, THEY COULD NOT SAVE THE RIGHT EYE, IT'S A DOUGHNUT IN MY VISION. GIVE ME COFFEE. DUNK IN DOUGHNUT. THERE ARE THINGS I MIGHT WANT TO TELL YOU B4 I PASS INTO THE NEXT WORLD. THE WORDS I SAY MIGHT HELP U DOWN THE ROAD. THIS IS MY CHANCE TO GET EVEN WITH YOUR MOTHER. I LOVED HER SO MUCH. IT'S TIME. I AM STILL HURTING FROM WHAT SHE DID TO ME. EVERY TIME I TALK ABOUT THIS WITH MY PSYCHIATRIST HE GIVES ME A HAPPY MEAL. MY PROBLEMS ARE WORTH A MILK SHAKE AND SIX BUCKS. SOMETIMES I EVEN GET A FIGURINE. MY PSYCHIATRIST TELLS ME I HAVE TO STOP BLOCKING THE DRIVE IN, IF I WANT TO RECEIVE HIS SERVICES. I SHOULD HELP HIM, SO HE CAN HELP ME. EVERYONE IN THIS WORLD IS IN IT FOR THEMSELVES. I YELL AT HIM OFTEN, BECAUSE I AM PAYING HIM WITH MY TAX DOLLARS. I YELL AT HIM OFTEN BECAUSE I AM GIVING HIM MONEY. YELLING AT HIM, I EXPLAIN TO HIM THAT I OWN HIM AND THAT ME BLOCKING THE DRIVE WAY IS A FILIBUSTER AGAINST THE BIG CORPORATIONS WHICH HE IS CLEARLY IN KAHOOTS WITH. WHATEVER HAPPENED TO HONEST BUSINESS?

I YELL AT MY CLERK PSYCHOLOGIST HEMATOLOGIST DOCTOR DOCTOR MISTER PRESIDENTAL. I YELL AGAINST THE POWERLESSNESS THAT IS ME. I YELL AGAINST THE BILLS THAT I HAVE TO PAY AND THE FRUSTRATION THAT IS MY LIFE. THIS USED TO BE A GREAT COUNTRY WHEN YOU HAD A MIDDLE CLASS INCOME. THIS USED TO BE A GREAT COUNTRY WHEN SUBURBIA WAS NOT INHABITED BY THE POOR. THIS USED TO BE A GREAT COUNTRY WHEN THE MIDDLE CLASS INCOME WAS NOT A WORKING CLASS INCOME. THIS USED TO BE A GREAT COUNTRY WHEN WE STILL WERE ABLE TO DISCERN SLEEPING BAGS FROM GARBAGE BAGS, PEOPLE FROM TRASH ON THE STREET. THE ECONOMY HAS REINVENTED THE CONCEPT OF 'EQUALITY BEFORE THE LAW'. WE ARE ALL SUBJECTS TO THE ECONOMY. WE ARE ALL DISPOSABLE INCOME NOW. MOVE THE MONEY AROUND.

MAYBE IF WE ALL JUST BOUGHT AMERICAN, WE, THE LITTLE PEOPLE, WOULD FINALLY OWN AMERICA. BUT MAYBE THAT IS ONLY A DREAM. IS THIS WHAT WE ARE BUYING INTO, A DREAM? I WANT OUT BUT CAPITALISM DOES NOT WANT ME OUT, BECAUSE THIS IS WHERE IT DOES NOT EXIST. DO YOU BELIEVE IN GOD? I OWN HIM BECAUSE I PAY FOR HIM WITH MY TAX DOLLARS. THAT IS WHAT I CALL MY INCOME TO GIVE IT SOME MORE MEANING, TAX DOLLARS. AND BECAUSE I PAY THEM TO GOD, HE HAS TO SPEAK FOR ME.

THAT'S WHY YOU GOT BIBLE LESSONS. BECAUSE I PAID FOR THEM. FOR WE ARE THE CHOSEN PEOPLE, SON. NEVER FORGET THAT. I AM NOT IN GOOD SHAPE. A LOT OF PAIN 24/7 THEY CANNOT INCREASE THE OPIOIDS BECAUSE MY BLADDER WILL NOT WORK. THE WORLD IS FILLED WITH SHIT. DUNK IN DOUGHNUT.

MAYBE ONE DAY YOU CAN FIND SOMEBODY TO PAY YOU MONEY TO SAY THOSE SAME WORDS TO SOMEONE YOU LOVE. IT HELPS TO HAVE A SYSTEM THAT REAFFIRMS YOU NO MATTER. THAT IS WHAT LOVE IS AFTER ALL. AND YOUR MOTHER NEVER GAVE IT. SHE ALWAYS HAD TO CRITICIZE.

NEVER FORGET HOW MUCH I LOVE YOU SON. NEVER FORGET HOW MUCH I LOVE YOU. DAD

—Daniel Schulz—

The Fox Thru Winter
—Tinamarie Cox

—Tinamarie Cox—

On the Lookout for the Butcher

—Tinamarie Cox

I've been keeping one eye on the road ahead,
and the other
is looking out for the butcher,
the blade that arrives to trim the fat away,
tries to make me perfect,
something more delectable for the plate.
But what I've failed to see
is that the fingers around the knife's handle
were always mine.

—Tinamarie Cox—

Bedroom of Want

—Isaac Salazar

—Isaac Salazar—

THE MOON AND THE CURING OF MY O. C. D.
—Daniel Flore III

I used to be scared
about cigarettes

about whether they
were out or not

I had Phil over
and with his big thumb

he crushed out his smoke
as he talked in awe about the moon

so I learned to just use my thumb
put it out and forget about it

now if only I could find
something in the moon

The Rubberband Girl Comic

—The Pink Zombie Rose Project – Dia & Beppi

—The Pink Zombie Rose Project – Dia & Beppi—

KATER

You first experienced it when you were 11. You & your sister claimed the finished attic for yourselves. You only had to clean it out (& cut the old noose from the rafters.) Dad didn't expect you to go for it, but you worked on the project for weeks, only to discover that the attic was actually really quite nice, & not at all haunted. You hauled twin mattresses up the narrow curving stairs. The low angular walls got two coats of paint—pale pink—& your sister painted the dormers glossy lavender. Becca hung posters: Kate Bush & Stevie Nicks.

Stevie Nicks

BECCA

2

Finally, at the very end, the last thing left was simple enough. It was only a loop of old fibrous rope, frayed & rotting from too much time. You dragged a slatted chair & Becca stood on her tiptoes. You handed her a pair of scissors. That close. Except you stretched all the way across the room. Your sister's mouth widened into a scream—O—but the sound was delayed. When Becca dropped the scissors, you hurtled back to yourself with a zipping sound like a retractible cord. Dad was a smug bastard, but he hadn't mustered the courage to cut that willful loop.

—The Pink Zombie Rose Project – Dia & Beppi—

You feel the power of the trees. You taste the nectar in the flowers. You hear the stars. You know their language; you feel the translation inside yourself, where you're still stardust. You're not held in place by space or time. You're not even YOU anymore. You're just part of the great becoming. The dissolving ego is replaced by cosmic unity. You take up yoga. You get the handle of it almost immediately. You understand how it all works. The universe. Your mind isn't cluttered like before, crowded with societal, directives, app passwords or expiration dates.

The yoga instructor takes you to her guru. Apparently, your birth was foretold by a flock of paper cranes. You are asked to teach a class. You do the standing tree & the child's pose. Attendants are brought to tears by the symbolism. Some remnant of you is left on earth, a burning ember of ego, & you cling to it. It's the red hot rock that keeps you from floating away. Your husband gets very angry. He stomps around the house. He says...

WHO DO YOU think you are, fat buddha incarnate?

It may well be true. You could be Buddha's current vessel.

The truth is, you don't know what you are. A rubber band?

—The Pink Zombie Rose Project – Dia & Beppi—

Magical Happenings Acknowledged in the Future
After Christopher Brean Murray
—Steph Patterson

Nessie will be recognized as a protected species.
She is still miffed about how people thought
she was a smudge in the pictures.

Spell books will replace burn books.

Bloody Mary will start a podcast
asking people to stop calling her
through the mirror.
It's all very exhausting.

Fairies will picket and ask people
to stop trampling their fairy rings,
lest those people never be heard from again…

Mermaids will join the call for climate change protection.
People that throw trash into the ocean
will be led to the sirens sans earplugs.

Dragons will travel to space
to see what other treasures
they can acquire
Beyond the earth's
barriers.

—Steph Patterson—

repentance, the decrepit thing
—Jessica Thiru

> *woke up screaming with no sound*
> *Ocean Vuong, Night sky with exit wounds.*

my father's screaming caught my legs
    like a bird's neck between a curious child's hands
it felt like I was running backwards
    into the mouth of a shore
my lungs almost overflowing with salt water
every bone in my body
    a worn out mercy
my father's screaming stained my ears with something best described as
    my mother's sorrow.

the boy wailing from my father's terror stood still
    alive but dying, naked in indecency.
his bleeding-a decrepit thing.
I knelt at his feet like I was praying
    a futile prayer
having been shun from faith by faith itself.

even in my sleep my heart hung around my neck
    like swaying pendant.
there's a type of hell in my throat
    I don't want to discover
the way it held my tears down
    with no hands
(even in my sleep).

how come I feel most when dreaming?

If lack of love is a sin
    god, how we need forgiveness
I've never really understood repentance
   but I feel I've grown hungry for it
we all have.

—Jessica Thiru—

Biographies

Robert Allen lives in Oakland, CA with his family, where he writes poems, offers workshops, and coaches poets to be better in their craft. More at www.robertallenpoet.com.

Shane Allison was bit by the writing bug at the age of fourteen. He spent a majority of his high school life shying away in the library behind desk cubicles writing bad love poems about boys he had crushes on. He has since gone on to publish four chapbooks of poetry *Black Fag, Ceiling of Mirrors, Cock and Balls, I Want to Fuck a Redneck, Remembered Men and Live Nude Guys,* as well as four full-length poetry collections, *I Remember* (Future Tense Books), *Slut Machine* (Rebel Satori Press), *Sweet Sweat* (Hysterical Books), and most recently *I Want to Eat Chinese Food Off Your Ass* (Dumpster Fire Press). He has edited twenty-five anthologies of gay erotica, and has written two novels, *You're the One I Want* and *Harm Done* (Simon and Schuster Publishing). Shane's collage work has graced the pages of *Shampoo, Unlikely Stories, Pnpplzine.com, Palavar Arts Magazine,* the *Southeast Review, South Broadway Review, Postscript Magazine* and a plethora of others. Allison is at work on a new novel and is always at work making a collage here and there.

James Asava (He/Him/His) is a biracial photographer and artist who specializes in alternative processing methods and ideas of identity. He chooses to work with these ideas to express how his culture has been stripped from him from growing up in predominantly white communities.

Andi Benet [they|them] is a lens-based artist based out of San Francisco. Disabled and queer, their art is focused on questions of perception and identity, featuring dreamlike, distorted imagery and their own body in performative self-portraiture. You can find them online at https://andi.love and @andiBenet on Instagram.

Sarah Blakely (she/her) is a poet from the Central Coast of California. She primarily writes trauma poetry and has self-published two trauma collections, *Volcano Girl* and *Scarlet & Shadows.* She is passionate about writing about women's rights and sexual assault awareness. She has also been published in the *365 Days of COVID* anthology by Sunday Mornings At The River, two anthologies (*Not Ghosts But Spirits* vol. 1 & 2) by Querencia Press, *From The Waist Down* by Papeachu Press, as well as *Issue #6 of Zimetra* magazine.

Jaimee Boake (she/her) is an Alberta based new mom, English Language Arts teacher. She loves reading, writing, spending time with her dogs, and is happiest, always, in the mountains. Winner of the Martyn Godfrey Award for Young Writers, her work has been published in multiple literary magazines and anthologies. Find her on Instagram @jaimeeannethology

Ace Boggess is author of six books of poetry, most recently *Escape Envy.* His writing has appeared in *Michigan Quarterly Review, Notre Dame Review, Harvard Review, Mid-American Review,* and other journals. An ex-con, he lives in Charleston, West Virginia, where he writes and tries to stay out of trouble. His seventh collection, *Tell Us How to Live,* is forthcoming in 2024 from Fernwood Press.

Catherine Broadwall is the author of *Water Spell* (Cornerstone Press, forthcoming 2025), *Fulgurite* (Cornerstone Press, 2023), *Shelter in Place* (Spuyten Duyvil, 2019), and other collections. Her writing has appeared in *Bellingham Review, Colorado Review, Mid-American Review,* and other journals. She was the winner of the 2019-2020 COG Poetry Award, and a finalist for both the 2021 Mississippi Review Prize in poetry and the 2021 Pinch Literary Awards in poetry. She is an assistant professor at DigiPen Institute of Technology, where she teaches creative writing and literature.

C.W. Bryan (he/him) is a student at Georgia State University. He lives with his clowder of cats (the best to ever do it) and girlfriend in Atlanta, GA where he writes poetry and short fiction. He is currently writing daily poetry prompts with a friend of his at poetryispretentious.com.

Joseph Byrd's work has appeared or is forthcoming in *Punt Volat, Pedestal, South Florida Poetry Journal, DIAGRAM, Clackamas Literary Review, Many Nice Donkeys,* and *Novus Literary Arts.* He's a Pushcart Prize nominee, was long-listed for the Erbacce Prize, and was in the StoryBoard Chicago cohort with Kaveh Akbar. An Associate Artist in Poetry under Joy Harjo at the Atlantic Center for the Arts, he is on the Reading Board for *The Plentitudes.*

Cyrus Carlson is an abstract painter from the Midwest

Ell Cee (*They/She*) is a lifelong artist as well as a member of the LGBTQIA2S, genderqueer, and disabled communities. They create one-of-a-kind, vibrant, and glowing art because ✦ joy ✦ . Ell uses recycled materials in much of their art, such as cardboard boxes, packaging materials, repurposed labels, and even discarded library books. Her art ranges across mediums: from watercolor markers, paints, pencil, photography, mixed-media, hand lettering, to pen & ink, and high resolution image conversion processes. Ell draws inspiration from stories, fairy tales, mythology, song lyrics, and nature. Her art embraces color and movement, showcasing the beautiful ways they can interact. Ell's art has been published in *Remington Review, Harbor Review, Pink Apple Press*, Zoetic Press's *NonBinary Review, On-the-High Literary Journal, Scavengers Literary Magazine, Writers Resist, The Uncoiled*, and as cover art for author James Jacobs. Find Ell's art online at https://linktr.ee/EllCeeTheArtist and @EllCeeTheArtist on Instagram.

Jillian Clasky is a writer from Toronto. She currently lives in Ottawa, where she's studying English and creative writing. Her work has appeared or is forthcoming in journals such as *PRISM international, flo.,* and *Rust & Moth.*

Ellen Clayton (she/her) is a poet and mother from Suffolk, England. Her poetry has been published in various online and print publications, including *Brave Voices magazine* and *The Hyacinth Review*. Her debut chapbook, *Home Baked,* was published in April 2022 by *Bent Key Publishing*. Ellen has performed her poetry at The Soho Theatre and the East Anglian Storytelling Festival and her work has been featured on BBC Upload. More of her writing can be found on Instagram @ellen_writes_poems.

Shannon Clem (she/they) is a queer, neurodivergent, disabled poet residing with their daughter in California. Their work is published or forthcoming in various journals & anthologies including *Beaver Magazine, The Hunger, Anti-Heroin Chic, Bullshit Lit, Warning Lines, & Not Ghosts, But Spirits Vol. III* (Querencia Press). Find Shannon on Twitter & Instagram @shannontantrum & www.shannontantrum.com.

Sara Collie (she/her) is a writer and poet based in the east of England. She has a PhD in French Literature and a lifelong fascination with the way that words and stories shape and define us. Her work explores the wild, uncertain spaces of nature, the complexities of mental health, and the mysteries of the creative process. Her poetry and prose have appeared in *Neon Door, The Selkie, Confluence, Synkroniciti, Stonecrop Review, Full Mood Magazine,* and elsewhere.

Frankie Concepcion is a writer from the Philippines and Massachusetts. She is an M.F.A. Candidate in Fiction at Arizona State University, and the current Managing Editor for Hayden's Ferry Review. She has received fellowships from Tin House, Sibling Rivalry

Press and the Virginia G. Piper Center for Creative Writing, and her writing has been published or is forthcoming in *Barzakh*, *StoryQuarterly*, *Joyland*, *HYPHEN*, and more. Her short story chapbook *Aftermath* is out now at Bottlecap Press.

Tinamarie Cox lives in Arizona with her husband and two children. Her writing and art have appeared in several publications in a range of different genres. She is also the author of a poetry chapbook, *Self-Destruction in Small Doses* (Bottlecap Press). You can find more of her work at: tinamariethinkstoomuch.weebly.com. And follow her on Instagram @tinamariethinkstoomuch and Twitter @tinamarie_cox.

Rachel Coyne is a writer and painter from Lindstrom, Mn.

Lori D'Angelo is a grant recipient from the Elizabeth George Foundation and an alumna of the Community of Writers at Squaw Valley. Recent work has recently appeared in *Beaver Magazine*, *Bullshit Lit*, *Idle Ink*, *JAKE*, *Litmora*, *One Art Poetry Journal*, and *Wrong Turn Lit*. Find her on the app formerly known as Twitter @sclly21 or Instagram and Threads at lori.dangelo1.

Chad Diamond Dann is a writer based out of the Pacific Northwest. His raw poetic style and open heart shows up in the words he writes in a completely authentic and unique way. His first book *The Pathfinder: The Journey of Becoming Yourself* is a Mini Memoir of his life leading up to the 2020 Pandemic. His second book *The Garden We Grow* is a collection of poetry & prose exploring the complex minutiae of the roller coaster we call life. Chad is also the owner of Grindstone Films a video production company focused on creating content for those making an impact in their community. Connect with Chad on IG & TikTok: @lionheartchad

Willow Page Delp is a Jamaican-American student, writer, reader, book reviewer and feminist buzzkill. Their work has been published by *The Lilac*, *The Indicator*, *News Decoder*, and *All Existing Literary Magazine*. They can be found on Instagram at @wxddo.

Fortune Simeon Eleojo is a Nigerian poet and short story writer. She attends Jewel Model School. In 2023, she appeared on the arts lounge climate change magazine. She receives support mentally from her mentor, Blessing Omeiza Ojo.

Gemma Elliott (she/her) lives in Glasgow, Scotland, and works in local government. She has published short fiction in *Neon*, *Idle Ink*, and *Divinations Magazine*, amongst others. Gemma can be found on Twitter and Instagram @drgemmaelliott.

Auguste Fallon (they/them) author of *"Demonic Trash Fire of Life"*, *"Zone Out"* and *"The Snail Lady"* and is an emerging multimedia artist, cartoonist, and educator who specializes in the creepy and cute. Born and raised in the Bay Area, Auguste holds a BFA in Cinema from San Francisco State University, while specializing in digital art and comics. They currently dwell in the wonderfully witchy Athena House of West Oakland with their partner and imaginary pet chimera. You can find them on all forms of social media at Occult Picture Show.

Zary Fekete grew up in Hungary and has a debut chapbook of short stories out from Alien Buddha Press and a novelette (*In the Beginning*) coming out from ELJ Publications. They enjoy books, podcasts, and long, slow films. Twitter: @ZaryFekete

—Biographies—

Dan Flore III's poems have appeared in many publications. His 6 poetry books are *Lapping Water*, *Humbled Wise Men Christmas Haikus*, *Home and other places I've yet to see*, *Pink Marigold Rays*,(Gen Z Publishing) *Written in the dust on the ceiling fan*, (Dead Man's Press Ink.) and *Hospital Issued Writing Notebook*.(Querencia Press)

Kevin Foote (he/him) is a writer, teacher, and explorer. He was born and raised on The Central Coast of California, but now calls Green Mountain his home. When he's not in class with his students, he loves investigating restaurants in the Denver region, trail running, and inviting friends and followers into the writing process with poetry through social media and poetry slams. His poetry has been published in *Beyond The Veil Press*, *Twenty Bellows Press*, and *South Broadway Press*, and he was the headlining poet at Mutiny Information Cafe in June of 2023. He is in the process of seeking publication of his first complete poetry collection, *Rivers*, a work full of the woe and wonder of teaching, the unsung moments of victory over mental health struggles, and the unabashed joy of experiencing the natural world along The Range. You can see his published poems and works in progress on his instagram page, @feastsonfoote

Emma Geller is a writer and interdisciplinary artist living in Boston, MA. She's known for her spooky aesthetic & commitment to rebelliousness. When she's not writing poetry, you can find Emma dancing alone in her room or playing her sticker-covered guitar. Her poetry and visual art has been featured in various publications, including *Quillkeeper's Press*, *Tabula Rasa Review* and *Goat's Milk Magazine*.

Michele Gorman (she/her) is a Michigan based writer, artist, and rescue dog mama. She uses vintage magazines and books to create her collages and believes that art, in all forms, has the power to heal.

andrea lianne grabowski is a midwestern lesbian writer occupying anishinaabe land. she appears in the inaugural issue of *Scavengers* and more of her published work lives in *The Ex-Puritan, Just Above Water: A Voyage YA Anthology, fifth wheel press, HELL IS REAL: A Midwest Gothic Anthology,* and elsewhere. she served as an editor for *NMC Mag* and is a Best of the Net nominee. you can find her making zines, on long drives being inspired by music, or peering in the windows of abandoned buildings.

Phillip Hatcher (he/him) is a Portland, OR based writer and avid Dnd player. He attempts to archive his life in all its little moments and when Atlas shrugs. Grasping from all manner of art, culture and history for inspiration, he hopes to pass on the passion for truly sucking the marrow from the bone. Published in Float On's: *Letters From the Void 2017,* Self-published: *A Knife Through Static 2021.*

Zoe Harvey-Prioleau is a talented 14-year-old woman residing in the vibrant city of Charleston, South Carolina. As a writer, she consistently brings her unique voice and perspective to the art of storytelling. Zoe, who prefers she/they pronouns, draws inspiration from her surroundings and personal experiences, infusing her writing with depth and authenticity. Growing up in Charleston, she finds inspiration in its rich history and diverse culture, which often serve as the backdrop for her captivating narratives. Zoe is supported and guided by her loving parents, who instill in her a strong work ethic and foster an environment where creativity thrives. Surrounded by two and a half siblings, she navigates the dynamics of a close-knit family, always finding solace and inspiration within those relationships. Through her writing, Zoe aims to challenge perceptions and share stories that resonate with individuals from all walks of life. The world eagerly awaits the literary masterpieces she continues to pen, as she paves the way for a new generation of artists and thinkers.

J.D. Isip (he/him) is the author of two full-length poetry collections, *Kissing the Wound* (Moon Tide Press, 2023) and *Pocketing Feathers* (Sadie Girl Press, 2015). His third collection, tentatively titled *I Wasn't Finished*, will be released by Moon Tide Press at the end of 2024 or early 2025. He is a contributing editor for *The Blue Mountain Review*. J.D. teaches at Collin College in Plano, Texas, where he lives with his dogs, Ivy and Bucky.

Annaliese Jakimides is a writer and mixed-media artist who grew up in inner-city Boston and raised a family on 40+ acres in northern Maine, growing almost all their food and pumping water by hand. Cited in national competitions and nominated for the Pushcart Prize and Best of the Net, her poetry and prose have been broadcast on Maine Public and NPR, and published in many journals, magazines, and anthologies, including *Beloit Poetry Journal*, *Solstice*, *A Dangerous New World*, *Maintenant*, *Utne Reader*, *GQ*, and *Breaking Bread*, the winner of two 2023 Maine Literary Awards and a Readable Feast Award. She is the cowriter of the musical *A Love Affair*, which will premier in 2024.

Ivy L. James (she/her) wrote her first story on Post-it notes as a child. Since then, she has graduated to regular paper and enjoys writing inclusive romance, short fiction, and poetry. She lives in Maryland with her wife and their corgi, cat, and two snakes. Website: www.authorivyljames.com

Jenna Johnson (she/her/hers), an Atlanta-based artist with a boundless creative spirit. Her artistic journey is driven by various mediums, but she finds herself most captivated by acrylic on canvas, alcohol inks, and the simplicity of pencil drawings. Drawing inspiration from the wonders of nature, Jenna weaves together vibrant plant life, celestial images, and marine life. Driven by her passion for self-expression and the ever-changing beauty of the universe, Jenna's creations invite viewers to witness depth of emotion and experience from different vantage points. Other works and endeavors can be found at www.pourlebonmotif.com and on social media.

Kenneth Johnson is a poet, visual artist, and educator living in Claremont, California. His work has appeared or is forthcoming in *The Diaspora/UC Berkeley*, *Carousel*, *Talking River Review*, *San Antonio Review*, and other publications.

S. Kavi (she/her) is a South Indian American poet, writer, and artist from Texas. Her work has been nominated for the Best of the Net anthology and appears in *antonym*, *Culinary Origami*, *Metachrosis Literary*, and elsewhere.

Karen Keefe (she, her) was one of the editors of *The Parlor City Review*. Her work is published *Anima*, *Anti-Heroin Chic*, *Silver Birch Press*, *unstamatic*, *Poetry as Promised*, *Wild Roof Journal*, *POETiCA Review* and the anthology, *F#ck the Patriarchy*.

Carella Keil is a Canadian writer and digital artist. "The House on the Hill" is part of her fairytale series, this one depicting Jack and Jill. Her work has appeared recently in *Columbia Journal*, on the covers of *Glassworks Magazine*, *Colors: The Magazine*, *Frost Meadow Review* and forthcoming on the cover of *Straylight Magazine*, as well as in *Chestnut Review*, *Door is a Jar*, *FVR Truthtellers*, Querencia Press, *Not Ghosts But Spirits*, and the first issue of *Scavengers*. instagram.com/catalogue.of.dreams   twitter.com/catalogofdream

Judge Kemp, Jr. (he/him) is a community-oriented leader living in Portland, Oregon. Diversity and inclusion are the core principles that drive and motivate him. His passions lie in connecting and bringing people together through events, writing, storytelling, collaboration, and being a positive philanthropic presence. As a leader, he believes in knowledge sharing as a way for empowerment and fostering an inclusive environment where everyone can be authentic and be fully engaged. A graduate of Portland State University, Judge majored in Communication Studies and minored in Community Development. He has served on the boards for Q Center (LGBTQIA2S+ community center) in Portland, the Oregon Commission on Black Affairs, and Portland's Red Dress Party. Prior to moving to Portland more than twenty years ago, Judge lived in Amsterdam, NL (Holland). He speaks Dutch, German, English, and is currently working on learning Spanish. Judge resides with his husband and life partner, home designer, Eric Schnell. They enjoy traveling, meeting new people, and entertaining friends at their home in Portland, OR. Judge is the blogger of <u>Judge Don't Judge...Much</u>, where he regularly posts about various topics of concern such as social (in)justice, LGBTQAI2S+ issues, and is the author of <u>Live. Love. Leo.</u>, a collection of semi-biographical poems.

Rose Kendall is a designer and illustrator originally from Scotland. Much of her work is inspired by nature and she loves a limited colour pallet challenge.

J.I. Kleinberg is an artist, poet, and freelance writer, she lives in Bellingham, Washington, USA, and on Instagram @jikleinberg. Her visual poems have been published in print and online journals worldwide and were featured in a solo exhibit at Peter Miller Books, Seattle, Washington, in May 2022, and displayed at the 2022 Skagit River Poetry Festival and in *The Cutting Edge: Art of Collage* in Asheville, North Carolina, in April 2023.

Dallas Knox (they/them) is a proud Tennessean and a junior at the University of Chicago studying religion and gender & sexuality. They enjoy going to the Art Institute of Chicago with their lovely girlfriend and watching the same movies over and over again.

Seth Kronick is a poet and journalist from Southern California. He currently writes for *TrillMag!* as a Creative Writing student at CSU, Long Beach. He is also a member of the Haiku Society of America. Seth's poetry has appeared in journals such as *Trash Panda*, *Frogpond*, *Poetry Pea*, *Vita Brevis Press* Anthologies: "Brought to Sight and Swept Away" and "Nothing Divine Dies", *Hearth and Coffin*, *Same Faces Collective*, as well as *Papers Publishing* among other publications.

Alysa Levi-D'Ancona is the author of the chapbook *An Absurd Palate* (Querencia Press 2023). She was born in Trieste, Italy, grew up in Chicagoland, and lives in Seattle, Washington with her husband and two polydactyl cats. She received her MFA in Creative Writing and Poetics from the University of Washington Bothell in 2023, and she teaches high school English by day. Liminality, surrealism, burlesque, absurdism, and speculative fiction are the pepper of her pages; stories, coffee, cooking, hikes, and blankets are the salt of her earth. Levi-D'Ancona's writing can be found in *Blood Tree Literature*, *Occulum*, *Stone Pacific*, *Alice Says Go Fuck Yourself*, *Cream Scene Carnival Magazine*, *Caustic Frolic*, and more.

LindaAnn LoSchiavo, a four time nominee for The Pushcart Prize and native New Yorker, has also been nominated for Best of the Net, the Rhysling Award, and Dwarf Stars. Elgin Award winner "A Route Obscure and Lonely," "Women Who Were Warned," IPPY Award nominee "Messengers of the Macabre" [co-written with David Davies], "Apprenticed to the Night" [UniVerse Press, 2023], and "Felones de Se: Poems about Suicide" [Ukiyoto Publishing, 2023] are her latest poetry titles. Forthcoming: "***Past Tense: Poems and Portraits of Suicides***." She is a member of SFPA, The British Fantasy Society, and The Dramatists Guild.

Syd M is a POC non-binary Arab American experimental artist that loves to try different mediums and express themselves that way. Their work is often inspired by their favorite bands and artists.

Gerald Majer is the author of *The Velvet Lounge: On Late Chicago Jazz*, published by Columbia University Press. They also are author of the poetry collections *David Murray Plays the Holland Tunnel* and *fountainous*. This year they completed the literary nonfiction book, *The Vibe Notebooks*. Their work has appeared in *Callaloo, Georgia Review, Puerto del Sol, Quarterly West, Vol. 1 Brooklyn,*

Yale Review, and other journals. They live in Baltimore and New Mexico where they pursue a range of collaborative experimental music and theater projects, including, with Baba L' Salaam, the sound-art duo Vibranium Experiments.

Liv Merritt is a poet living along the front range of Colorado. Merritt's poetry viscerally explores themes of nature, human emotion, and entropy. When not writing, Liv pursues other creative endeavors, collecting bones, and spending time with their cat, Mr. Toad.

Skylar Miklus is a poet living in Durham, NH. They obtained their B.A. in Philosophy from Dartmouth College and are pursuing their MFA-Poetry at the University of New Hampshire. Their poems have appeared or are forthcoming in *Defunct Magazine, Assignment Literary Magazine, new words {press}, Scavengers Literary Magazine*, and elsewhere. You can find their work at https://skylarmiklus.wixsite.com/portfolio

Roya Motazedian (they/them) is a nonbinary poet/writer born in the Netherlands, raised in England, and currently residing in Hamilton, Ontario. Their parents were born and raised in Iran. With so many countries tied to their history, they spend their time writing poetry about being on the 'borderline' of everything: genders, cultures, teenagehood/adulthood, and more. Home, in particular, is a huge keyword for them. Their work has appeared in *Incite Magazine, The Melange, Kiwi Collective Magazine*, and *Dark Thirty Poetry Publishing's anthologies*. You can find them on instagram, @milkdippedsky.

Rachel Mulder lives in Portland, Oregon, with her two cats, Opal and Tomasina. She was born in rural Wisconsin and when she was small she spent a lot of time sitting in the grass staring, obsessing about animals, watching cartoons and peeling her skin off. Now she makes drawings using a variety of media that often yield printmakerly textures - residual effects from earning her BFA in Printmaking at Milwaukee Institute of Art & Design in 2007. Encouraging others (and herself) to create/exist sincerely is a parallel passion of hers that braids itself into her visual work.

Abigail Ottley lives in Penzance. Her work has appeared in more than 250 outlets including *Sylvia Magazine, The High Window, Trigger Warning, The Survivor Zine.* A contributor to the *Invisible Borders (2021)* and the *Duff (2022),* she was twice Highly Commended in Frosted Fire's Pamphlet Award (2023) and won the Wildfire Words Flash Fiction competition later the same year. She writes poetry and short fiction,

Tiffany Overby lives in Portland, Oregon. She is inspired by the natural world around her and the practices of gratitude and observation.

Melissa Palumbo (she/them) is a 24-year-old writer based in Arkansas and has written poetry for most of her life, with themes including nature, society, and identity.

Steph Patterson (she/her) is a poet from Delaware with a love of dark fantasy and horror. She lives with her family in their cozy home by the creek. She spends her time creating magic with words, dreaming up ways to smash the patriarchy, and rewriting old fairy tales. Her work was recently featured in the 2023 Poem of Day from *Gnashing Teeth Publishing*. You can find her on Instagram: @spatterspoetry

Bernard Pearson has published two novels, Where *Willows End* and *In Red Blood*, with Leaf by Leaf press He Lives in Oswestry.Shropshire U.K . He is a published poet, spoken word performer, finalist in the *John Tripp Spoken Word Competition* and *The All Wales Comic Verse Competition.* He is also a biographer and prize-winning short story writer. His poetry has appeared in many publications, including; *Aesthetica Magazine* and *The Edinburgh Review,* In 2017.a selection of his poetry 'In Free Fall' was published by *Leaf by Leaf Press*. In 2019 he won second prize in The Aurora Prize Poetry Competition.

Kushal Poddar is the author of 'Postmarked Quarantine' has eight books to his credit. He is a journalist, father, and the editor of 'Words Surfacing'. His works have been translated into twelve languages, published across the globe. Twitter- https://twitter.com/Kushalpoe

Michael Putorti is an artist who specializes in both linocut printmaking as well as drawing, his practice often striving to combine the two. He holds a Bachelor of Fine Arts Degree in Art as well as a Master's degree in Art History and Visual Culture. He creates works of art depicting a variety of subject matter, ranging from still lifes, landscapes, and portraits of humans and as of late, animals. His reason for creating my prints really comes down to two reasons. The first reason is because he simply loves the process of carving into linoleum and bringing details to life, whether through block printing ink or colored pencils. His second reason is to help address and educate his viewers on a variety of subjects we face in the world today. For example, his ongoing series "Anthropocene" focuses on several endangered species and strives to demonstrate the beauty of these creatures who face numerous challenges to their lives.

Monique Quintana (She/Her) is a Xicana from Fresno, CA, and the author of *Cenote City* (Clash Books, 2019). Her work has appeared in *Maudlin House, Wildness, Lost Balloon, The Acentos Review,* and other publications. She has been supported by Yaddo, the Sundress Academy for the Arts, the Kimmel Harding Nelson Center, and the Community of Writers. You can find her at moniquequintana.com. Instagram and Twitter: @quintanagothic

Sage Ravenwood is a deaf Cherokee woman residing in upstate NY with her two rescue dogs Bjarki and Yazhi. She is an outspoken advocate against animal cruelty and domestic violence. Her work can be found in *The Temz Review, Contrary, Pioneertown Literary, Grain, Sundress Press anthology - The Familiar Wild: On Dogs and Poetry, The Rumpus, Lit Quarterly, PØST, Massachusetts Review, Savant-Garde, ANMLY (Anomaly), River Mouth Review, Native Skin Lit, Santa Clara Review, The Normal School, UCity Review, Janus Literary, Jelly Bucket, Colorado Review, Pangyrus, PRISM International, 128 Lit, A Gathering of the Tribes, Ponder Review, Shō Poetry Journal, MORIA, Indianapolis Review,* and more. Her book, *Everything That Hurt Us Becomes a Ghost* is forthcoming from Gallaudet University Press in October 2023.

Kristiana Reed (she/her) is a bisexual writer and the Editor in Chief for *Free Verse Revolution*, a literary & arts magazine. Reed often explores the body, illness, addiction recovery and womanhood through the natural world and written portraiture.

Adrianne Reig (she/her) has work published in *All Existing Literary Magazine* and *Atlantis Magazine*. She is based in coastal North Carolina.

K.G. Ricci is a self-taught NYC artist who has been creating collages for the past seven years. In that time his work has evolved from the larger 24x48 panels to 7x10 books and most recently to a series of 11x14 collages on cardboard titled Incongruities. His work has been in gallery exhibitions throughout the country, and he has appeared in numerous on-line exhibitions. Many of Ken's most recent "visual stories" have been featured in several literary magazines.

Angeleen Rohda (she/her) is a writer based in the greater Minneapolis/St. Paul area of Minnesota and shares her work on sagesandpages.com. She has a bachelor's in Communication with a written specialty from St. Catherine University. Professionally working as a marketing manager, she spends her time reading, writing, playing outside, and binge-watching TV – winters are long in the upper mid-west. As an adoptee and Black bi-racial woman, family, and race are common topics for her to explore.

Alex Rodberg (she/her) is a multifaceted storyteller/artist who weaves captivating tales through various artistic mediums. With an insatiable passion for creativity and a profound love for mixed media, Alex uses emotions, experiences, and dreams to connect with viewers in various forms. Drawing inspiration from life's intricate tapestry, she loved to create art that transcends traditional boundaries, often merging the realms of visual art, literature, and media in a way that resonates with audiences.

Pink Zombie Rose Project: As Beppi scanned **US** magazine's "Celebrities are just like US" in line at the local 7-11, she was always grateful that visual artists didn't have to worry about this injustice. No matter how many gallery shows she had under her belt or how many periodicals her comics/artwork appeared in- there would be no paparazzi lurking in the shadows waiting to catch her looking slap-dash devouring a Big Bite. However, as Beppi learned years ago when she appeared on Artworks This Week, visual artists are still subject to those Bette Midler in Beaches moments of cringe. "Beppi feels things very deeply." Currently, Beppi is illustrating a series of comics from writer Dia Van Gunten's Pink Zombie Rose. Here's to Dia finding the right safe word! Dia is Cream Scene's EiC and the demented mind behind the Pink Zombie Rose series. (one of them.) She unleashed an undead apocalypse on her hometown of Toledo, Ohio and now the author's got nothing left for bios, but she needs to up her game if she's gonna keep pace with Beppi. She used to get cute— "Dia is 6 persimmons" or "Dia a blue envelope with a sticky lip. " —but it made her look pretentious, which of course she is. That's just another word for nerd. The safe word is cockatoo. Cockatootletoo!

Nayt Rundquist (they/them) is an award-winning anthologist; writer of weird things; editor of best-selling books; and professor of creative writing, literature, and publishing courses. Their odd scribblings can be found in *Inverted Syntax*, *Digging Through the Fat*, *Roi Fainéant*, *X-R-A-Y Lit Mag*, *Fast Flesh Literary*, *The Citron* Review, and anthologized in *Unbound: Composing Home* (New Rivers Press 2022). They live just outside space and time with their artist-jeweler wife and their fifth-dimensional dogs.

Mubarak Said, TPC XII, is the SprinNG Alumni,a reader at the *White Cresset Arts Journal*, the winner, March edition of the *Threposs* poetry contest and the 3rd runner-up, poetry category of the 2022 Bill Ward Prize for Emerging Writers. He was longlisted in Gimba Suleiman Hassan esq poetry prize, and also a guest contributor at Applied worldwide, US. He is a member of Jewel literary and creativity foundation and Hilltop creative arts foundation. His works are forthcoming from and published in *World Voices Magazine*, *Brittle paper*, *Eboquills*, *Icefloe Press*, *Literary yard*, *Beatnik Cowboy*, Wellerism, Teen Literary Journal, new feathers anthology, ILA magazine, the yellow *magazine*, *ariel chart*, *Afrihill*, *arts lounge*, *Icreative*, *piker press*, *madswirl*, *imspired magazine*, *Pine Cone Review*, *Double speak Magazine*, *Memory house Magazine*, *Sink Magazine*, *Aural magazine*, *Arting arena*, *Synchronized chaos*, *Susa Africa*, *culture cult press*, *south broadway press*, *thebezine magazine*, *williwash*, *hot-pot magazine*, *peppercoarst lit*, *Literary cocktail*, *Applied Worldwide*, *Opinion Nigeria*, *Today Post*, *Daily Trust* and elsewhere.

Isaac Salazar is an Austin-born and Houston-based multidisciplinary artist. His work has appeared in *orangepeel*, *Cathexis Northwest*, and *The Acentos Review*. He is a graduate student at Rice University.

Daniel Schulz (he/him) is a U.S.-German author, academic, factory worker, and Pushcart Nominee for 2022, known for his publications in journals such as *Fragmented Voices, Word Vomit, A Thin Slice of Anxiety, Dipity, Flora Fiction,* the catalog *Get Rid of Meaning* (Walther König 2022), and his editorial debut *Kathy Acker in Seattle* (Misfit Lit 2020). His chapbook *Welfare State* and *No End to Abuse* will be published by Book Room Poetry at the end of 2023. IG: @danielschulzpoet

Nolo Segundo, pen name of L.j. Carber, 76, in his 8th decade became a published poet and essayist in over 150 literary journals and anthologies in 12 countries. The trade publisher Cyberwit.net has released 3 poetry book-length collections: *The Enormity of Existence*

[2020]; *Of Ether and Earth* [2021]; and *Soul Songs* [2022]. A retired English/ESL teacher [America, Japan, Taiwan, Cambodia], he has been nominated for the Pushcart Prize and Best of the Net.

Anna Louise Steig is a young Jewish writer currently studying creative writing and business at Shepherd University in West Virginia. Follow her for life and literary updates on IG @a.l.steig

Julie Stenton is a writer, poet, and artist agent based in Sydney, Australia. She is the author of the poetry collection, *In the Dream I Jump From a Great Height and Land Safely*, published by indie press Sunday Mornings at the River. In her work, Julie often tackles themes of identity and belonging, and is known for her emotive and thought-provoking writing. She enjoys sandwiches (chicken), birds (oystercatchers), and shapes (triangles). In a sense, she is already long gone and forgotten, which frees her up a great deal for being alive.

Liam Strong (they/them) is a queer neurodivergent cottagecore straight edge punk writer who has earned their BA in writing from University of Wisconsin-Superior. They are the author of the chapbook *everyone's left the hometown show* (Bottlecap Press, 2023). You can find their poetry and essays in *Impossible Archetype* and *Emerald City*, among several others. They are most likely gardening and listening to Bitter Truth somewhere in Northern Michigan. Follow Liam on Instagram and Twitter: @beanbie666

Irina Tall (Novikova) is an artist, graphic artist, illustrator. She graduated from the State Academy of Slavic Cultures with a degree in art, and also has a bachelor's degree in design. The first personal exhibition "My soul is like a wild hawk" (2002) was held in the museum of Maxim Bagdanovich. Writes fairy tales and poems, illustrates short stories. She draws various fantastic creatures: unicorns, animals with human faces, she especially likes the image of a man - a bird - Siren. In 2022, she took part in Poznań Art Week. Her work has been published in magazines: *Gupsophila*, *Harpy Hybrid Review*, *Little Literary Living Room* and others. In 2022, her short story was included in the collection *The 50 Best Short Stories*, and her poem was published in the collection of poetry *The wonders of winter*.

Emily Tee (she/her) writes poetry and flash fiction. Nature, environment and society, as well as ekphrastic writing, often feature in her work. She's had recent pieces published in *Unbroken Journal*, *Free Verse Revolution Lit*, *Gypsophila Zine*, *The Ekphrastic Review*, *Visual Verse* and *Aurum Journal* with poems upcoming in print with *Dreich Mag* and elsewhere. Emily lives in the UK.

Betty-Jo Tilley is a Los Angeles-based writer whose critical work and interviews have appeared in *The Coachella Review*. A June 2023 graduate in fiction and nonfiction from the University of California at Riverside Low Residency MFA Program, she is currently at work on a novel.

Jessica Thiru (she/her) is an 18-year-old currently living in South Africa. She graduated from high school in December of 2022, and is currently studying Financial Sciences at the University of Pretoria. Jessica has been writing fairly consistently since the age of 16, and her passion for the art has grown exponentially since. She aspires to, in the near future, work as an author and editor herself. Aside from writing, she finds pleasure in playing piano, reading, watching anime, and taking care of animals. Born and raised by Kenyan parents she moved a lot as a kid. In an ideal world, she would travel enough to have a home nowhere in particular.

Tawnya Torres lives in the Pacific Northwest wonderland near the ocean. Her debut novel is a fantasy romance. *A Silent Discovery* came out in October 2022 followed by her science fiction romance *The Heart of the Machine* which was released in March 2023. She thought she would be a horror or mystery writer but it's the love story that captivates her. Right now, she works in a cute bakery and cafe but hopes to someday be a full-time author and move to Hawaii.

Samantha Tucker (she/her) is an educator, writer, yogi and new mother based in Bristol, UK, navigating her way in the world. A lover of long walks and cups of strong tea, she is always eager to explore new places, throw her shoes off and take a dip in water.

Emily Ruth Verona is a Pinch Literary Award winner and a Bram Stoker Awards® nominee with work featured in *Under Her Skin, Lamplight Magazine, Mystery Tribune, The Ghastling, Coffin Bell, Rust + Moth, The Jewish Book of Horror, Monstrous Futures,* and *Nightmare Magazine* among others. Her debut thriller, *MIDNIGHT ON BEACON STREET,* is expected from Harper Perennial in 2024. She lives in New Jersey with a small dog.

M.J. Walker lives in the south west of England far from the hustle and bustle of the city. She writes short fiction to clear her mind of the head-bugs that bite in the night.

Lauren Emily Whalen (she/her) has creative nonfiction published or forthcoming in *Blue Mesa Review, Jabberwock Review,* the Querencia Press Spring 2023 Anthology and *Write or Die.* She has studied the craft of personal essay with Chloe Caldwell and Isaac Fitzgerald. Lauren's fourth novel *Tomorrow and Tomorrow,* a New Adult reimagining of Shakespeare's *Macbeth* co-written with Lillah Lawson, will be published by Sword & Silk October 2023. Follow her on Instagram @laurenemilywrites or visit laurenemilywrites.com.

Franchon Whitby's writing explores everyday moments of life, love and family, capturing both the significant and trivial moments in keen detail. She lives in Los Angeles, where she was born and raised. Her website is: lalanative.com

Robin Williams: Author, short film director, spoken word album producer, femme who makes god quiver… there is nothing Robin Williams, a queer poet from Pennsylvania, can't do. They've written the chapbook *GIRL.*, published with Querencia Press, and *wild honey,* self-published, and have had previous publications in the *Horizon Literary Magazine, Moss Puppy magazine, Warning Lines* magazine, *Free Verse Revolution* magazine, and many more. When not tormenting the patriarchy, Robin can be found watching Little Women for the four-hundredth time or spending time outdoors with her family of eight cats. Instagram: @paperbackfern
Website: www.greenferncoven.com

Elaine Westnott-O'Brien is a writer and teacher of English language and literature. She writes in all forms, and her work has appeared in *The New York Times, Querencia Press* and *Papeachu Press,* among others. She has recently been awarded a mentorship by the Munster Literature Centre with the award-winning poet Afric McGlinchey. She lives with her wife and two children in Tramore, Ireland. Find her on Instagram @elainewob_words.

Kristin Yates is an award-winning poet, artist, cat cuddler, and work in progress from Lewisville, North Carolina. Her poems have appeared in *Tiny Seed Journal, Beyond the Veil Press, Writerly Magazine, Unstamatic, Campfire Poets,* and others. She can be found at: https://www.instagram.com/beautefantasy/

www.ingramcontent.com/pod-product-compliance
Lightning Source LLC
Chambersburg PA
CBHW081106300726
48976CB00010B/2679